ISBN 0-373-44064-2

HIS BODYGUARD

Copyright © 1999 by Lois Greiman

All rights reserved. Except for use in any review, the reproduction or utilization of this work in whole or in part in any form by any electronic, mechanical or other means, now known or hereafter invented, including xerography, photocopying and recording, or in any information storage or retrieval system, is forbidden without the written permission of the publisher, Harlequin Enterprises Limited, 225 Duncan Mill Road, Don Mills, Ontario, Canada M3B 3K9.

All characters in this book have no existence outside the imagination of the author and have no relation whatsoever to anyone bearing the same name or names. They are not even distantly inspired by any individual known or unknown to the author, and all incidents are pure invention.

This edition published by arrangement with Harlequin Books S.A.

® and TM are trademarks of the publisher. Trademarks indicated with ® are registered in the United States Patent and Trademark Office, the Canadian Trade Marks Office and in other countries.

Printed in U.S.A.

HIS BODYGUARD
Lois Greiman

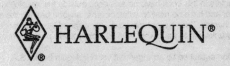

HARLEQUIN®

TORONTO • NEW YORK • LONDON
AMSTERDAM • PARIS • SYDNEY • HAMBURG
STOCKHOLM • ATHENS • TOKYO • MILAN • MADRID
PRAGUE • WARSAW • BUDAPEST • AUCKLAND

What Inspires Me...

Being raised on a North Dakota cattle ranch, I grew up with an appreciation for all things country—from animals to wide open spaces to country music. So this book was a very natural step for me. It's peopled with the kind of characters I love—people with close family ties, a solid idea of what is truly important and a flavorful sense of the ridiculous.

His Bodyguard was a joy from beginning to end. I hope you have as much fun reading it as I did writing it.

—Lois Greiman

To Cary Bardell—
the most selfless person I've ever met.
Thanks for being there for me
more times than I can recall.

1

"SURE. I'LL GET A BODYGUARD." Nathan Fox rose from behind the table of The Cowboys' tour bus and thumped his coffee cup onto the counter. "Soon as hell freezes over."

"Dammit!" Sarge Bartel swore with feeling. "I don't work my butt off just so you can—"

"Hey," Paul Grand interrupted. Dressed in nothing but a pair of loose shorts, he glanced up from behind his newspaper. "Looks like you'll have to be hiring someone then, Nate. 'Cause it says here that it was twenty below zero last night in North Dakota. Isn't that where you're from? Hell, North Dakota?"

"That's *Hill!*" Nate corrected.

Paul Grand may have the unerring timing of a superstar drummer, but he had the tranquil soul of a hermit. His love of music, and not his thirst for fame, had brought him here. He was the inevitable peacemaker amongst The Cowboys. That quality, however, had never convinced Nathan to treat him with more dignity than he did anyone else unlucky enough to cross his path.

"Hill, North Dakota! Shows what you know of God's north land, you confederate traitor," Fox said and turned toward the door. But he stopped in midstride. "Geez!" He started slightly, then bent for a better view between the window's narrow blinds. "Where'd that crowd come from? And a banner. Paul..." He squinted as if reading. "Paul Grand...Fan Club! No kidding? Hey, Paul," he said and turned toward the table, but the drummer was already crouched behind his paper like a whipped cur, his face pale and his baby blues round.

"What?" he rasped.

Nate glanced out the window, then back. "Well, it ain't more than a dozen or so folks. But they're heading this way. 'Less you want to greet them in your boxers, you'd best pull on some jeans, son."

Paul jerked to his feet, backed stiffly toward the wall, and tripped over a tawny, oversized cat who yowled in outrage and shot for the bedroom.

"You're joking!" Paul wheezed.

Nathan shook his head once, turned toward the window, then back with a shrug. "Well…yeah, guess I am."

"Bloody hell!" Paul sagged against the wall like linguini that had failed the test. "Someday that sick sense of humor's gonna get you killed, Fox."

Nathan drew in the sweet sight of Paul's humiliation and chuckled. "My mom always said, never kid a kidder. That's *Hill*, North Dakota." He removed his hat for a moment to place it reverently over his heart. "Home of the free and the brave."

"Bloody hell," Paul repeated, but weakly this time, his Kentucky accent barely discernible as he melted back into his chair. "Don't get him a bodyguard, Sarge. If someone's got it in for him, they sure enough got their reasons. Let 'em at him."

Nathan replaced his hat and headed through the bus's mini-kitchen. "You kidding? My fans love me." He stopped at the door. "And you know why?"

Silence. At the back of the bus, Jimmy Fry wandered groggily from the sleeping quarters.

"Because I'm just a damned nice guy," Nate said.

It was a quote so old no one remembered who had said it the first time. But Nate pretty much held the record for repeating it since.

"Shut up, Fox," said the boys in tired unison.

Nathan ducked outside with a grin.

The heat of the morning sun struck him like the kick of a mule. Okay, he didn't necessarily long for the subzero temperatures of home, but a little breeze might be nice. How did these southern guys breathe down here?

"Hey!" Sarge yelled, following him. "We're not done with this!"

Nate kept walking. The heels of his Justins rang on the concrete and his huge team-roping belt buckle shone in the sun as he strode toward the hotel. "I told you, Sarge. I don't need a bodyguard."

"And I told you. Either you get yourself some security or you get yourself a new manager."

"Consider yourself fired then," Nate said and stepped into the hotel.

Sarge snorted as he edged through the door, his ever-present clipboard in one brawny hand. "Yeah, and who'll interview the new recruits?"

"Thought you'd do that," Nate said, striding down a hall-way.

"And who'd hire my replacement?"

"You."

"And who'd clean up the mess when the new guy screws up?"

"Guess that'd have to be you, too," Nate said.

"Damn right!" Sarge agreed. He turned belligerently at the door to the small conference room they'd rented and scowled at Nate. "I didn't mind giving up the spotlight so you could become a damned country idol, Fox, but I've made this band work and I ain't about to let you—"

"Not this again!" Nathan groaned and reached for the doorknob, but Sarge blocked the door with a beefy shoulder.

"You ain't going to get yourself snuffed out while I'm running the show."

"Snuffed out?" Nate leaned back on a slanted heel and failed to hide his grin. "You know what the shrink said 'bout you reading them Sam Spade books, Sarge."

"I've showed those letters to the police. They don't think death threats are so funny."

"The police don't think anything's funny, Sarge. If they have a sense of humor, they get tossed off the force."

Sarge's scowl deepened, causing more wrinkles to form below his flattop haircut.

"It's the truth. Saw it on *Cops*," Nate said and reached for the door again.

Sarge knocked it shut. "Goddamn it, Fox!"

Nathan groaned, removed his Stetson, and wiped the back of his hand across his forehead. "Geez, it's hot down here."

"Damn straight," said Rover, just passing by with a foam cup of coffee. "Back home we'd still be shoveling snow." The whites of his eyes were a distinct shade of pink, and he looked like he'd slept under a truck somewhere, but for a guitarist he was pretty steady. Of course, guitarists were judged differently than normal people. Still, he'd been around from the beginning, long enough to remember what it was like to freeze their butts off pitching manure during a frigid North Dakota winter. It made the travel, the Mississippi heat, even the lack of privacy, a little more tolerable.

"Listen," Nate said, remembering, with some nostalgia, when Sarge sang lead and used to crack a grin now and then. "I'll give the bodyguard thing some thought. But I've got an interview with a lady from the *Catfish Journal*. Heard she's a looker." He sighed. "It's a tough job, but… You know. 'Fraid I don't have time for a bodyguard just now."

"That's what you said last month," Sarge reminded, his tone testy.

Nate grinned as he pulled the door open. "That don't make it any less true," he said and took a step inside.

But when he glanced around, his smile faded. He stepped back out and let the door close behind him.

"Sarge?"

"Yeah?" Sarge's tone had turned from testy to nasty.

"Why are there a dozen men with fat necks in there?"

Sarge's blond brows were low over his icy blue eyes, and his chin, Nate noticed, jutted forward like the jaw of a bulldog on steroids. "Because I told them to come."

"Why?"

"Because you need protection."

Nathan Fox ground his teeth. Why had he decided to become a musician? He could have been anything—a sidewalk caulker or a guy that makes galoshes...or a pig farmer. He'd always liked pigs. "Listen, Bartel," he said slowly. "I'll tell you what I need. I need some time off. I need a full-time cook, and I definitely need a girl just like the girl that married dear old Dad. What I don't need is a bodyguard."

"The hell you don't!"

Nathan glanced through the window, then ducked back and grimaced. "Geez, they look like they've come for a damned funeral. Only, they haven't decided whose yet."

"Then hire one of them, so it ain't *yours.*"

"And what about my interview?" Nate asked.

"She'll wait."

"Where is she?"

"She'll wait," Sarge repeated.

They glared at each other for a moment.

"You're one pushy bastard," Fox said.

"And it's made you a pile of money."

Nathan considered arguing that point. After all, he'd like to think he had something to do with his own success, but Sarge *had* started the band. It had been his own decision to eventually slip into a managerial position. He was, Fox had always admitted, first-rate at the job. Unfortunately, he was about as personable as sandpaper.

"What do I have to do?" he asked.

"Just go in there, talk to 'em, let me know which one suits you."

"None of them suit me. You choose."

"And have you spend the next six months complaining about my choice? Not hardly. I know you better than that."

But not well enough to realize just how much this entire situation irritated Nate. He knew he should do something about the security problem. But dammit, it was bad enough that he had to hire someone to drive his bus, book his gigs, and answer his mail. Now he needed someone to protect his person? Just because a couple of guys were bored enough to send him a few crank letters? What was next? Someone to floss his teeth? Chew his food? Cut his toenails? It was too much, taking away another little piece of his independence. Taking away another piece of himself.

"You want out of it, just say the word." Sarge's voice was low. Not for a moment did his icy gaze shift from Nathan's face. "Maybe it ain't worth it to you no more." His posture was stiff and there seemed to be almost a breathless hopefulness in his tone. For the first time in over a decade together, Nathan wondered if *Sarge* had had enough.

"You don't have to keep at it, you know," Nate said.

"You saying *I* should quit?"

"I know you've been pretty stoked up about things."

"And you're not at all worried?"

"They're just letters."

"And the accidents?"

Nathan shrugged. The motion relieved a bit of his own tension but seemed to do nothing for Sarge. "Just accidents. Sure no reason to pull out."

Silence stretched taut between them, but in a moment Sarge reached for the door.

"Then I guess I got my job cut out for me," he said, and motioned Nathan inside.

The perimeter of the room was lined with chairs that seemed to groan beneath the weight of the applicants. The fellow to Nate's immediate left had a neck like an Angus bull and an expression that was only slightly less friendly. Not that Nate was intimidated. It didn't matter if the guy was beefier than he. But the fact that his *eyeballs* were more muscular was a little unnerving.

Geez, if Tyrel heard his little brother had hired someone to protect him from his adoring fans, he'd laugh his butt off. Not to mention his father, who thought musicians just slightly less masculine than say…ballerinas.

Sarge stepped toward the center of the room. "Thanks for coming," he said. Nate noticed that his dour expression nicely matched the others in the room. "My name is Sarge Bartel. I'm the one who sent for you this morning. And this here is Nathan Fox." He nodded toward Nate. "You probably recognize him. And since he's the one who's famous, he's the one needing a bodyguard. So I'm going to have him do the hiring.''

Nathan glanced around at the square faces, the belligerent expressions, the bulging jackets. Perfect—if he were inclined to hire a hit man.

But the thought of inviting one of these guys to join his crew was ludicrous! Sarge must be kidding. But one glance at his manager assured Nate that that unlikely incident had not occurred.

If it weren't so sad it would be damned hilarious.

Nate cleared his throat. ''Good morning.'' It seemed strange suddenly—he could entertain a crowd of thousands without breaking a sweat but felt totally at a loss with this hairy-knuckled lot. ''We've had a few security problems recently. I guess that's why you're all here.'' He cleared his throat again, feeling foolish. Old Angus neck was staring at him with an unwavering gaze. It gave him the creeps. ''So I guess we'll have to beef up security.'' He eyed the Angus's meaty neck and grinned at his own pun. When he was uncomfortable he had a habit of telling jokes, and when he told jokes he had a tendency to get in trouble. Still, that would be preferable to standing here like an idiot with the tension bubbling like boiled pine tar. ''So I've decided to throw you all in the ring together and let you duke it out. The survivor's got himself a job.''

The room went absolutely still. A few men turned their eyes aggressively to their neighbors, and one brute actually cracked his knuckles.

Tough crowd, Nathan thought. But suddenly he heard a tiny sparkle of laughter. It wasn't the deep-throated chuckle of Arnold Schwarzenegger, but the sweet, quicksilver giggle of a woman.

Nathan swiveled quickly about. And there she was, sitting just to the right of the door, her strawberry lips tilted and her eyes bright.

Green. Green eyes, he decided. Like a spring meadow. And her legs…they were as long as a Dakota January and as slim as hope, with her nyloned knees pressed together just so.

She was like a light in a very dark place. He smiled. She smiled back, her expression a mixture of apology and humor.

Nathan leaned toward Sarge. "I want *her*," he said with a sigh. He knew he was being facetious, knew that somehow his interviewer had snuck in here after all. He also knew that her presence would irritate his bossy manager no end. Sarge liked everything just so. He frowned on spontaneity and hated practical jokes. "Always have a backup plan" was his mantra.

His clipboard, in fact, might be considered his closest friend, and got the lion's share of his quality time. Even now, it sported a list of names that were neon color-coded in highlighter and marked with a certain number of stars.

Nathan turned to him now, waiting for his disapproval. But all of Sarge's attention was focused on the woman.

Silence filled the room, then, "Maybe we should all introduce ourselves," Sarge said, his tone intense. "Let's start over on this side." He nodded toward the woman, his gaze never wavering. Fascinated, Nathan turned his attention back to her.

Her hair, upswept and held in place by the kind of magic only women knew, was the color of a chestnut colt's. She wore a silk, lime-colored blouse that buttoned down the front. Her golden tan made him speculate whether it went clear to her toes. Just about now he'd give half a year's income to find out, and screw the interview.

"I'm..." She paused for just an instant. "B. T. O'Shay." Her accent could be called nothing but cute, Mississippi thick and down-home adorable.

"O'Shay?" Sarge flipped a page over on his clipboard and skimmed a column of names. When he lifted his head, his eyes were gleaming. Sarge was not one to appreciate surprises. "You're B. T. O'Shay?"

Nathan hadn't thought she could sit any straighter, but she managed it somehow, though the top of her head barely reached the ear of the fellow to her right.

"Yes, I am," she said, a hint of defiance in her drawl, her teeth milky white against her palomino tan.

It took a moment for the reality of the situation to sink into Nathan's sweltering brain, but when it did, he smiled. He was one lucky bastard. She was here for the job as a security officer, a person hired to be at one's side night and day. They did do night work, didn't they? But, of course. They would have to, and the idea of this little bit of femininity shadowing his every move sent a giddy tide of glee spurting through him.

This was great. Not only could he avoid hiring a *real* bodyguard, he could pay this luscious little package for her company, *and* piss Sarge off at the same time. Judging by his manager's darkening expression, he was not overjoyed to see little Miss O'Shay sitting there proper as a schoolmarm and determined as a road mender.

"You're B. T. O'Shay from Bartman Security?" Sarge asked. He said it as if he was certain the girl had somehow forgotten her own name and foolishly assumed someone else's identity.

Nathan upped the wattage of his smile. It wasn't that he was insecure about his masculinity, he assured himself, but why would he want to be followed around by one of these steroid-hungry brutes when he could be spending time with *her!*

"That's correct," she said. "I've been working for Bartman for nearly a year now."

"A year. Wow," Nate said. "Any of your clients been killed yet?"

She cleared her throat and gave him the corner of a heart-stopping smile. "So far we've brought 'em all back alive, Mr. Fox."

The way she said "Mr. Fox" made him go weak in the knees. "Hear that?" he asked Sarge, and raised his brows as if impressed. "Not a single casualty."

His manager stared at him for a moment, then scowled at the next applicant. "Your name?" he asked.

"Fields. Frank Fields, sir."

Sarge flipped his page back. "From Stirling Security?"

"Yes, sir." He kind of barked his answer.

"And how long have you been employed there?"

"Five years, sir." Woof.

Nathan happily turned his attention back to B. T. O'Shay. What did the B. stand for? Brenda? Bridget? Bambi? He liked the name Bambi. It conjured up images of soft and cuddly, nestled in his arms like a sleepy lamb. He'd always liked lambs.

"And before you worked for Steele?" Sarge was asking.

Why was she here? Nate wondered. Could it all be a hoax? Might she be masquerading as a bodyguard just to get an exclusive interview with him? Stranger things had happened. Once he'd found a reporter hiding under his hotel bed. He'd never been sure how she'd gotten in there, but it had been really quite interesting getting her out.

"I was a Marine, sir."

Or maybe she was just a fan. She'd been collecting pictures of him for years and when she'd heard he was coming to Jackson, she had hatched up this scheme to meet him. If that was the case, he had to admire her ingenuity and reward her tenacity.

"And you?" Sarge asked, moving on to the next man.

"Kevin Anderson. Three years with Warrior Security. I was a personal guard for Madonna when she was here in town."

"You don't say."

"Yeah. She said I had great…technique." He followed his statement with a suggestive chuckle, but Nathan barely noticed.

Bambi's eyes were very large—much like the famous fawn's. She wore a narrow ivory-colored skirt and beneath that were legs like a thoroughbred filly.

"Greg Taylor. Lionheart Corporation. Top of my platoon at Survival Plateau."

The freckles sprinkled across her nose made her look like the perfect girl next door. Someone who might have grown up with the Beaver.

"Davey Braun. Kingpin Corp."

She wore a small string of pearls around her throat, which was long and slim and appeared kissably soft.

"Mac Greenley. Be Safe Security. Graduate of Guardsman Inc. Heavyweight wrestling champion of Tennessee."

Her face was lovely, and her waist was tiny. But, generally speaking, it was somewhere in between those two regions that fascinated him. Brother Tyrel was a leg man, but Nathan himself had always appreciated softer regions. He almost sighed as he eyed her bosom, which, though not large, made his heart do funny things in his chest.

Maybe she was a singer, desperate for a break and willing to pretend to be a bodyguard to get his attention. Fact *was* sometimes stranger than fiction. And as it stood, he was more than willing to pay her just to quiet Sarge and keep these hired mastiffs off his scent. Hell, he'd gladly let her sing backup if she was any good. And after that…

"Did you hear that?" Sarge asked, sending Nate a glare. "Heavyweight champion of Tennessee."

"Yeah," Nate said. "Can I talk to you, Sarge?"

"Sure."

"Outside?"

Sarge's brows lowered farther. "They haven't all been introduced yet."

"Fido can wait," Nate murmured and turned toward the door.

Sarge followed.

The hall was very quiet. Nate allowed himself one glance through the window at the angelic redhead, then turned his attention back to his manager.

"Hire O'Shay."

Sarge's eyes glinted in the absolute silence. "What?" he said in a voice so low it was barely audible.

Geez, Nathan loved ticking Sarge off. He couldn't help it. It was in his nature. But he really was a damned nice guy. Kind of. So he didn't smile when he said, "Hire O'Shay," again.

"The girl? You want me to hire the girl?"

Against Nate's better judgment a sliver of a grin escaped his control. "That's right. I want her on the payroll today."

"You're out of your mind."

"Me?" Nate did his best to look shocked. "She works for…" He glanced at Sarge's list. "Bartman Security. A two star company."

"I didn't know she was a woman when I called her in."

That much was obvious. Still, Nathan reared back as if surprised. "Sarge, you're not saying you're a chauvinist are you?"

"You want out of the limelight so bad, just say so. You don't have to get yourself killed to do it. But if you want to hang around, you'll get yourself a real—"

"Bodyguard. I know," Nate said, raising one hand. "You've been saying all along I need more security, and one glance at her made me see the light. I absolutely need someone to guard my body, and she's the one for the job."

"You don't know a damn thing about her."

"Not true. She's oh, say five foot four, green eyes, red hair, about 34-23-34, and I think I saw a tiny little mole…" He motioned toward his own chest. "On her right breast."

"Let me tell you something, smartass. I'm not about to march in there and hire *anyone* without a thorough interview."

"Well…" Nate sighed, removed his Stetson, and ran splayed fingers through his hair. "Have it your way then. Interview away." Replacing his hat, he tilted it back and added, "Then hire Bambi."

2

BRENNA THERESA O'SHAY SCREAMED, leapt into the air, and kicked the hanging dummy directly in the head. It twisted like wind chimes in a hurricane, swung madly toward the ceiling, and snapped off its chain.

Brenna winced as it crashed against the far wall, but remained warily on the balls of her feet, still in position, every muscle ready, lest her enemy retaliate. Not surprisingly, it did not, but scowled from its crooked position in the corner. She relaxed, bowed to her long-suffering opponent, and reached for the towel that hung over the bar in her basement workout area.

She was primed. She was ready. She was a lethal weapon. She was a killing machine. She was…terrified.

Sweet Mary! What had she done? She wasn't a bodyguard, built up on testosterone, steroids, and centuries of male pattern aggressiveness. She was a receptionist for a local security company. She weighed little over a hundred pounds, barely topped five feet four inches, and hadn't been entrusted with guarding so much as the lollipop supply at Bartman Security.

But none of that was through any fault of her own, she reminded herself. It wasn't as if she hadn't asked Roger to give her assignments. She had. In fact, she'd taken the job at Bartman with the understanding that she would eventually be given active duty.

She should have figured out long ago that wasn't going to happen. She should have known when Roger said how good she looked behind the desk. She should have known from the way the men eyed her legs. They all knew she would never advance beyond the tight rein of the reception area. Regardless of her efforts, regardless of her accomplishments, there didn't seem to be a man alive with a modicum of faith in her abilities.

Until she'd met Nathan Fox.

A flicker of fragile hope glowed in Brenna. Finally, someone had taken her seriously. Finally, someone had seen past her gender to the steel within.

True, she still felt guilty for keeping Sarge's phone call a secret. She could get in a lot of trouble for that. But she couldn't sit behind a desk forever and watch her dreams be worn away by time and frustration. She was twenty-three years old, and she knew what she wanted from life. True, as a child she'd wanted to be a cowboy, and as a young adolescent she had been pretty sure she'd make a top-notch jewel thief. But in her heart, she'd always known the truth; she was meant to be in law enforcement. It was in her blood, in her genes, passed down to her like her curly red hair and her Irish temper. She may have inherited her mother's fair skin, but she had her father's resolve.

Sarge Bartel's phone call had been a catalyst for her, kick starting her imagination. What if she didn't tell anyone about the interview? What if, instead, she went herself?

It had been her boss who had finally convinced her to go. When, in guilty agony, she'd asked him again when she could expect active duty, he'd told her not to fret about it. She was getting a raise at the end of the month, because he wasn't about to lose the best damned coffee maker in Mississippi.

She hadn't kicked him in the gut like she'd wanted to. She hadn't raved at him. She hadn't even given him a nice ladylike chop at the base of his neck.

Instead, she'd returned to her desk, called Sarge, and assured him that Bartman Security would be sending one B. T. O'Shay for the interview in two weeks.

With her course set and her heart racing, she'd gotten down to business—not pumping iron, but pumping her brain.

She'd spent hours poring over articles about the man the country-and-western tabloids called "The Fox."

She'd learned everything from his hat size to his personality—size 7½, and charismatic enough to charm "the skin off a copperhead," as one Arkansas woman had written.

Brenna had taken notes, made copies, and filed away a hundred tidbits of information in her mind. After compiling a small mountain of data, she had endlessly debated how best to approach the interview, agonizing for hours over what to wear, how to talk, walk, shake hands, blink.

For two entire days she had tried on clothes at local men's shops, donning everything from pinstripes to fatigues. The truth had hit her like a roundhouse kick to the kidneys. She looked like nothing more than an effeminate Mugsy Malone. She might make Nathan Fox laugh in that kind of getup, but she wasn't likely to impress him with her macho masculinity.

No matter what she did, every other applicant was certain to look tougher than she. All would probably have impressive backgrounds, and a few might even have training superior to her own. She couldn't beat them at their own game.

She'd redoubled her studies, and in a tiny article in an outdated copy of the *New York Times,* she'd learned the most interesting tidbit of all. It stated in Nathan's own words that while, yes, he was concerned about his safety, he did not want a bodyguard who would follow him around like some slavering bulldog. He wanted a normal life, or at least as normal as a superstar could hope for.

After that a definite plan had begun to gel in her mind.

It had taken her three more days to choose her outfit. But instead of pinstripes and derbies, she now considered pearls and pumps.

And it had worked! It had paid off! Nathan Fox had hired her, had realized the kind of courage it took for a woman to compete in a man's arena, had understood the confidence necessary to wear a skirt into a room where the testosterone was as thick as Mississippi mud.

In short, he had recognized her talent.

"Miss O'Shay."

Fox's smile hit Brenna with the intensity of Southern sunshine. Though she had assured herself it wasn't possible, he really was better looking in person than in photographs. And being here in his hotel suite, knowing he'd slept in the next room, added a risqué factor to the meeting that bumped up her heart rate another notch.

"Mr. Fox," she said and took his hand, remembering to shake it hard enough to convey confidence, but not so hard as to seem defensive.

The most difficult part was over, she assured herself; she'd already met with Sarge. He hadn't looked happy about the prospect. Instead, he'd maintained a sort of smug satisfaction as he'd signed the contract stating that she was in the employ of Fox Inc. and that the company would pay her directly.

So far her silk jacket, chosen after only two hours of silent debate, remained sweat free.

"It's good to see you again." Fox's voice was as melodious as she remembered. A journalist in Vermont had said his eyes were the color of maple syrup. But that was just sappy drivel, because they were a full shade darker than that, closer to the color of fresh-ground coffee beans, and they crinkled charmingly at the corners when he smiled, mesmerizing her with their warm allure.

"Would you like some breakfast?"

"Oh." She drew her hand self-consciously from his embrace, realizing she'd been staring. If she screwed up this opportunity she could just nail her butt to an office chair, because she wouldn't be leaving it anytime soon. "No, thank you. I'd best get straight to business."

"Right now? It's only…" He glanced at his watch. His wrist was broad and corded, sprinkled with dark hair. "Eight o'clock. On the dot." He winced. "You're not always this prompt, are you?"

"I try to be."

"Yeah." He cleared his throat, then turned and motioned her to go with him. "Me too," he said, and pulled the door open to usher her through. "I'm supposed to go running at eight o'clock."

"I read you're a runner."

"You read about me?" He sounded flattered. Odd, she thought. He was, after all, adored by millions. Surely he wasn't surprised that she, too, knew something about him.

She made the mistake of glancing up at him to see if he looked sincere. The brilliance of his smile momentarily numbed her brain, but she bludgeoned it back into working order. "Yes. I thought it wise to read a couple of articles." A couple *hundred*. After all, walking into that interview cold and landing the job was just about as likely as a snowstorm in Georgia. "I always try to learn as much as possible about my, uh, clients before I begin working for them."

"You didn't read that I'm an immature prankster, did you? 'Cause it's definitely not true. I would never send a critic chocolate-covered laxatives."

"You did that?"

"Uh...no," he said. "Why do you ask?"

She laughed. Despite his drop-dead good looks, he had a down-home way about him that couldn't help but put her at ease. "I'm afraid I didn't read anything negative. All the interviewers were women."

He chuckled and ushered her through the next door as she silently berated herself. She hadn't meant to say that. It implied, of course, that no female could possibly find fault with him. Although she suspected that might well be true, she certainly had no reason to give him the impression that *she* was amongst the infatuated group.

"Are you blushing, Miss O'Shay?" he asked.

She kept her face turned resolutely forward. There were a good number of things she appreciated about her heritage. Her complexion was not amongst them. "It's rather warm in here."

He laughed again. "Looks like I was entirely wrong about this bodyguard business. I like having you around already." He turned away, saying, "Table for two."

Brenna realized suddenly that they were in the hotel's restaurant. The hostess, a young brunette with big eyes and a ponytail, dimpled at him and turned away with obvious effort.

He ushered Brenna along with a hand on her back.

"I thought you were going to go running," she said.

"I said I'm *supposed* to go running. But I don't like to on an empty stomach."

"I'm the opposite." She slid into the booth across the table from him.

"I'll have coffee, black as you can get it. What'll you have?"

"Nothing, thanks."

"You gotta have something. Sarge said you were going to be asking me questions. You need fluids for that."

"I do?"

"Absolutely."

She shrugged. "Orange juice, I guess."

"Orange juice it is." He smiled up at the hostess. For a moment, Brenna was afraid the girl might swoon. A Chicago journalist had said that when Fox entered the room, all the oxygen was sucked out, which might have explained the vacuum-like quality of the restaurant. "And could you send our waitress right away? I'm starving."

"Yes sir."

The girl finally forced herself to leave. Across the aisle, two young women turned to stare at him. Brenna tried to ignore them and concentrate on the business at hand. She was going to have to learn to focus despite the distractions.

"So you like to run after you eat?" she asked.

"No. I…"

But just then the hostess reappeared, coffeepot in hand, flying from the kitchen as if summoned by the king of Sudan.

"Thanks," he said, then turned back to Brenna. "The way I figure it is this. I run down the road, right? I might be hit by a car, or die of a heart attack, or, hell…" He shrugged. Beneath the wear-softened cotton of his T-shirt, his shoulders looked muscular and lean. The word "perfect" popped into her head. She pushed it back out with effort. He was her *boss,* and she was certain to eventually learn that he had *some* faults. "Way things are, someone might drive by and shoot me in the head just for kicks." He took his first sip of coffee, smiled at the hostess and said, "Great stuff."

Her world complete, Miss Ponytail floated away on a cloud.

Brenna waited for him to complete his sentence, but he seemed to have forgotten his line of thought, lost as he was in caffeine bliss.

"And?" she said finally.

"And? Oh. And I don't want to die on an empty stomach."

She raised her brows and waited for him to say he was joking, but he didn't.

Instead, he gave her a self-effacing grin. "Sarge says I eat too much. Hell." He took another sip of coffee. "Everyone says I eat too much."

Now she knew he was kidding, for although she had looked, she hadn't detected a single ounce of fat anywhere on his body. In fact, he looked as fit and hard as one of her school friends' prize quarter horses.

The silence was getting lengthy. And she was staring again. She snapped her gaze away, resisted clearing her throat, and settled on fiddling with the pleats of her rayon slacks beneath the table.

"I'd like to thank you, Mr. Fox," she said, using her most professional tone. "Some—"

"Just a minute," he interrupted. A waitress was already hustling toward him. She was blond, buxom, and a little wide in the hips. As she panted up to the table, Brenna noticed that she looked about as unlikely to remain conscious as the last woman.

"Are you ready to order?" She sounded breathless as she looked Nathan in the eye.

Brenna silently thanked her CPR instructor for her thoroughness—just in case.

Nathan flipped open his menu, skimmed the items for a moment and began. "I'll have a steak, two fried eggs, a side of grits, an order of buttermilk cakes, a large glass of milk...and...how big are your buns?''

"What?"

He didn't look up, absorbed as he was in his selections. "Your sticky buns. How big are they?"

"Oh. They're big."

"I'll take two. No. Just one." He grinned at Brenna. "I promised Mother Sarge I'd cut down. And you?"

She couldn't help blinking at him. "Me what?"

"What'll you have to eat?"

"Noth—"

"Listen." He leaned toward her conspiratorially. "It'd be really nice if you'd eat with me, 'cause otherwise I'm going to look like a pig."

She felt a lock of crinkly hair fall over her forehead. She'd tried to subdue that hair with gel and a scrunchy at the back of her neck, but it remained stubbornly out of control.

"Please," he added softly.

A woman could drown in those darker-than-maple-syrup eyes of his.

"Okay." She yanked her gaze from his. "I'll have some toast," she said, glancing at the waitress.

Unfortunately, the blonde was in another dimension, her gaze locked on Nathan's profile.

"Miss?"

"Yeah?" The waitress jerked from her reverie, her eyes wide.

"I'll have some toast."

"Oh. Sorry. Sure. Are you Nathan Fox?" she blurted out.

"What?" Brenna said, but the other woman had already yanked her attention back to Fox.

"You're Nathan Fox, ain't ya?"

He smiled up at her. "Yeah."

"I got all your tapes."

"Really?"

"Yeah. If I..." Her face was red. Brenna shifted slightly toward the aisle, ready to catch her if she collapsed like an axed pine. "If I got one from my car would you autograph it?"

"I'd be tickled."

"Huh?"

"I'd like that," he said.

Amazingly, Brenna thought, he sounded sincere. What a guy! Too good to be true, stunning, talented, charismatic. And he was nice, with a butt as hard as... Her *boss!* Boss!

The waitress hurried away.

Brenna forced her gaze down to the table. She was beyond the age of hormonal overdrive. Besides, that sort of thing had never worked well for her anyway. Even without her brothers' constant interference, her love life had never been really phenomenal.

Pulling a notebook out of her purse, Brenna flipped it open and cleared her throat. "We'd better get started before she comes back. I need to know—"

"You were going to thank me."

"What?"

He smiled. A couple of brain cells melted on impact and sizzled into nothingness. "You said you were going to thank me for something."

"Oh." She glanced at the metal spiral of her notepad, then met his gaze. "For hiring me."

He was silent for a moment. "It was my pleasure. Believe me."

She was tempted to ask him why he had done it. What he had seen in her that all the other men in her life, her family included, had failed to understand. But that would surely not be professional. Best to pretend that she had *assumed* he would recognize her ability.

"I appreciate it," she said instead. "I won't disappoint you."

"I know."

Would throwing herself onto his lap and kissing him senseless seem unprofessional? Probably. "Well then...let's get started. I'll need to know what kind of security problems you've had in the past."

"Your order, Mr. Fox."

Brenna's jaw dropped as the waitress bustled up. She was loaded down like a pack mule, but still beamed as she kicked a stand into place and slid a heaping tray onto it.

"Hope that didn't take too long."

Too long? They had either cooked this stuff with a blow-torch or they'd stolen someone else's orders. Or more likely, they'd stolen *five* other people's orders.

"No. I hadn't even started gnawing on the table yet," Nathan said.

The blonde laughed. "I told Sharon it was for you."

"Sharon?"

"The cook. She's a fan, too. And she was wondering—"

"Bring me more butter and an extra cup of syrup and I'll autograph her stuff in blood," he said, eyeing the tray of steaming food.

"Really?"

"Well, no. But—"

"I mean…not the blood part, but will you sign hers too?"

"Sure. Soon as I'm done eating."

"Oh! Yeah!" She began sliding the food off the tray and onto the table. "There you go. Anything else?"

"The butter and syrup."

"Right." She hustled away.

Fox, already cutting up his steak, glanced up and grinned. "Good thing you got that toast so I don't look like an oinker."

She laughed, unable to help herself.

His fork stopped in midair. "You got a really pretty smile."

She sobered immediately, reminding herself with bubbly panic that her dream was on the line here—years of preparation, hundreds of hours of practice on the shooting range, the workout floor, in the classroom. She could not afford, under any circumstances, to be distracted by a handsome face.

"We'd better get down to work," she said.

"Right." He took a bite of steak, closed his eyes as if

concentrating, then opened them and nodded. "What did you want to know?"

"What kind of problems you've had in the past."

"Oh, well, my cholesterol's a little high. Don't know why. Could be 'cause of them midnight snacks. But, you know. We're on the road. There's nothing to do...."

"I meant *security* problems."

"Oh." He took another bite, washed it down with a gulp of milk and began mashing up his eggs. "None."

She stared at him. "What?"

"I've been really lucky. My fans are great. You want to taste these eggs? They're..." He took another bite. "Wow."

"But Sarge said you've been having trouble. Something about threatening mail."

Nathan waved at her with his fork. "Sarge is...Sarge. He doesn't sing with the band anymore. So he's got too much time to fret. There's nothing to worry about." The pancakes were beginning to disappear.

"Then why did you want a bodyguard?"

"I didn't," Nate said. "But Sarge insisted."

"Why?"

He shrugged. "There have been a couple of accidents. A few letters."

"Could I see them?"

"You don't need to worry about it."

She stared at him. A warning bell clanged in her head. Don't worry about it? As in, don't worry your pretty little head? Brenna forced herself to relax. There was no reason for her to get angry. Nathan Fox was, by all accounts, a good guy. Still, something had knotted in her gut, and the tension wouldn't go away until she'd learned the truth.

"Can I ask you a question, Mr. Fox?" she said, her lungs aching with tension.

"Sure."

"Why did you hire me?"

"You mean, why did I hire *you* or—"

"Why did you hire *me!*" She exhaled slowly, calming herself. But she had waited so long for this opportunity. Had put up with so much, had held her temper at Bartman no matter how many times "the boys" had complimented the fit of her blouse or the color of her hose.

When she'd met Nathan, she'd felt a flicker of hope. Losing that hope might well be the death of her dream.

"When there was a room full of men with more experience and far more bulk, why did you hire me?" she asked, dreading the answer, but needing to know.

"You laughed at my joke. I can't work with someone with no sense of humor."

She forced her muscles to relax. "So you really *do* plan to let me do the job."

He watched her as if trying to read her thoughts. "Hell yeah," he said softly. "You don't have to worry about that. You're already on the payroll. Guaranteed a job till the end of the tour at least. Sarge tells me it's an ironclad contract, so I better be sure."

That wasn't exactly what she had meant, but he seemed to think he had reassured her.

His eyes were warm, sincere, somber for once. "It doesn't matter why you applied for the job. All you have to do is hang around and keep Sarge happy." He took a swig of coffee. "And maybe, if you don't mind, we could take in a couple of movies or something."

Beneath the table, Brenna tightened her hands into fists and tried to breathe normally. "So you don't think you need protection?"

He paused for a moment, then, seeming unable to resist, grinned and said, "Oh, I always use protection, honey."

Her dream shattered like a porcelain vase. Rage flew up with the piercing shards. She jerked to her feet.

"My name is not honey," she rasped.

He rose more slowly, his expression befuddled. "I didn't mean to offend you," he said. "Fact is, I was wondering about your name. B.T. What does it stand for?" He stuck his hands into the pockets of his jeans, looking young and vulnerable. "It's not Bambi, is it?"

"Bambi!" She choked on the word. She had to get away,

had to leave, collect her wits…before she killed him. She spun around…and crashed into the waitress who was watching them, mouth agape.

Tapes flew in every direction. The waitress staggered backward, and Brenna, thrown off balance, careened sideways only to be caught in Nathan's arms.

He drew her slowly erect, his gaze locked on hers, his right arm tight about her waist.

"You okay?"

"I'm fine!" she choked.

His expression was sober as he watched her. "Listen. It don't matter why you're here. Maybe you're in some kind of trouble. Maybe you gotta get out of Mississippi. Maybe you need an interview." He shrugged, still holding her. "Truth is, I couldn't care less if you don't know a Winchester from a water pistol. I'm just happy to have you…" he tightened his arm slightly about her waist "…*here.*"

The rage turned cold. "Really?" she said, then leaned closer, hugging her arm to her chest.

"Really."

Her gun seemed to leave its arm holster of its own accord, and suddenly its barrel was pressed against his jaw as it pointed toward the ceiling.

"Well, it isn't a water pistol, Fox," she said through gritted teeth. "It's a semi-automatic, 40 caliber, blued Glock 27 with a 10-round magazine, and if I hear another hint of sexual harassment, it can blow your earlobes off from twenty-five yards. Anything else you'd like to know about personal handguns?" she asked, and behind her, the waitress fainted dead away.

3

THE BUS RIDE TO CHARLOTTE, North Carolina was interminable and tense. Despite Brenna's outrage at discovering Fox's latent chauvinism, she had neither killed him nor quit. Instead, she'd calmed down as best she could, then proceeded to do her job with all the dignity she could muster.

But just about now, her muscles felt like mush and her eyes as if they'd been sandblasted. Even so, she'd refused to remove her contacts, though she assured herself her reasons had nothing to do with vanity.

It was in the wee hours of Thursday morning when she finally stumbled out of the bus and onto the sidewalk. She'd survived for nearly a day and a half as a security officer. A day and a half of poring over the questionable letters Sarge had given her to read, of wondering whether the seemingly inconsequential accidents Sarge told her about were accidents at all, of ignoring the band's curious stares, of being hopelessly worn down by her own self-doubts.

Although The Cowboys had two buses, most of the band had ridden together. It gave Brenna the perfect opportunity to learn more about them, or so she had told herself. In actuality, she'd learned little more than their names—Paul Grand, the drummer; Jimmy Fry, the fiddler; Rover, the guitarist; and Brian Mueller, who played keyboard. Oh, and there was the driver called Atlas, and the cat, a gargantuan tom called Nuf. Other than that information, she'd gained nothing except for the beginning of an ulcer and a pounding headache.

The lobby of the hotel they trooped into was empty except for a balding fellow who stood behind the counter in a slightly shiny, one-size-too-small suit and a plastic rectangular badge that proclaimed him to be Gregory. Sarge pushed past the others, exchanged a few words with the man and came back to pass out key cards.

There were yawns and mutters as The Cowboys wandered groggily off.

"Thought you'd want the room next to Nate's," Sarge said, handing Brenna a key and staring at her for a moment.

"Oh. Thanks."

Sarge turned away, leaving her alone. Self-conscious, she lifted her overnight bag from the floor and stumbled up the stairs after the band.

The men filed off to their own doors, Nathan stopping before number 1026. Brenna remained where she was for a moment, but if there was ever a time to be assertive, now was it. Steeling herself, she stepped up to Nate's door.

"Here." Without glancing at his face, she slipped the key from his hand. "I'll do that." The plastic card slid into the slot. She turned the latch, pushed the door open, and stepped inside.

Nathan, however, remained in the hallway, his brows raised, and his head slightly canted.

She flipped on the light, glanced about the sitting room and motioned him inside.

He came, letting the door close behind him. But Brenna refused to look at his face. Instead, she hurried through the next doorway, glanced into the bathroom and assured herself there was nothing even vaguely threatening. Going on, she shoved open the closet door. Certain that small space was empty but for the usual apparatus, she continued into the bedchamber. The curtains were drawn shut, the bed perfectly made. All seemed quiet, but what seems and what is can be as different as a caterpillar from a butterfly. Master Leong, her judo instructor, had a propensity for expounding on such drivel. He had shared that tidbit of wisdom with her the first day a ten-year-old boy had effortlessly flipped Brenna over his head.

Striding over to the bed, she lifted the eyeletted dust ruffle and peered underneath. A walnut-stained board closed off the underside of the bed. She tapped it with the toe of her shoe, made certain it wasn't loose, then hurried around to the other two sides to do the same.

Turning toward the window, she swept the curtain aside. All was secure, so she paced back to the door. Nate remained where he was, his brows still raised as he stared at her.

"Making sure we're alone?" he asked, his lips quirking into the suggestion of a grin.

"Making sure *you're* alone," she corrected coolly and brushed past him to reach for the door handle. "Hook the security chain," she ordered and pulled the door open.

"What about the bathtub?"

She turned back to him with a scowl. "What?"

"You didn't check behind the curtain."

"There is no curtain. There are glass doors. You can see right through them."

"Yeah?" he said, and grinned slightly, as if he were thinking something lascivious.

The expression carved deep grooves into his tan cheeks and set his eyes sparkling. But he did not look sexy, she promised herself. Even though his T-shirt was pressed smooth over his chest and his faded jeans clung to his thighs like a possum on a limb, he wasn't the least bit appealing. Irritating was what he was.

She repeated that in silence and came up with a reasonably effective scowl.

He grinned, then paced to the bathroom and squinted inside as if nearsighted. "The glass is frosted. There might be someone in there."

"There's no one in there."

He twisted around to look at her again. "She might be really little."

Gritting her teeth, Brenna let the door swing closed and returned quickly to the bathroom. Pressing past him, she slid the tub door open and peered inside.

"No one," she said.

"Phew!" He shook his head and let his shoulders drop as if he'd been holding his breath. "That's a relief."

"Uh huh," she said, but when she exited the bathroom, he still hadn't moved, forcing her to brush past him again. She pursed her lips, refusing to acknowledge the spattering of feeling caused by the contact. "What time will you be leaving your room in the morning?"

"Gee. I hadn't decided," he said and stuck both hands into his back pockets. "What sounds good to you?"

That innocent act was hardly going to work on her. Not now that she knew his real reasons for hiring her. Not now that she knew he was a male chauvinist oinker who didn't believe in her abilities any more than the other men in her past.

"Call me as soon as you wake up," she ordered.

"What?"

She stopped at his shocked tone and turned to glare at him. "I need to know when you're no longer safely in your room. Call me before you open this door. I'll be in 1027."

"You mean..." He widened his molasses eyes as if shocked. "You're not going to sleep in here?"

Her jaw dropped. He thought... He believed...

But in an instant she saw the gleam in his eye. She gritted her teeth, but she couldn't stop the color that diffused her face.

"Hook the chain," she said and turned away.

"What about the window?"

"What?" she snapped, pivoting back around.

He stepped back as if frightened, but his grin was bigger now, not little boyish but full-blown. "You didn't check the window."

"Yes, I did."

He shook his head. "You just moved the one curtain a little. There might be someone hiding behind the other one."

She tightened her fists. Violence was never the answer, she reminded herself. But that old saw had never seemed less true. "If there was someone hiding behind the curtain, wouldn't he make a bulge?"

"Maybe it's a really tiny woman. Them little ones..." he eyed her up and down, as if noting her small size "...they can be tricky."

She opened her mouth to argue, but he raised a palm. "Sarge hired you in good faith. I'd hate to give Bartman Security a less-than-stellar report about you, B. T. O'Shay."

Brenna snapped her mouth shut. Bartman Security! Roger Bartman didn't know anything about this. In fact, she'd told her boss she was quitting, was leaving Jackson to marry a cotton farmer near Mobile. She'd gone to great pains to type up an official-looking contract that told Sarge she was to be paid directly. All was going smoothly—sort of. But if Fox called Roger all hell would break loose.

"I'll check the window," she said, and turning, marched across the room.

"I appreciate this, B.T.," Nate said.

Pushing the curtains aside, she glared at every inch of the wide panes. Everything was perfectly in place.

"By the way, what does the B.T. stand for?"

"You can call me O'Shay," she said coolly. In a moment she was by the door. She pursed her lips, waiting for him to speak again, but he didn't.

She turned the latch.

"Miss O'Shay?"

"What!" She jerked back toward him, her nerves stretched tight.

The right corner of his mouth quirked up in unison with one eyebrow. "Sleep tight," he murmured, and she fled.

INSIDE THE SOLACE of her own private room, Brenna paced. She must be out of her mind! What had made her ever believe she could be a bodyguard? And why in heaven's name had she chosen Nathan Fox's body to guard? He *deserved* to be attacked. Besides, he resented her very existence. He was never going to accept her presence here. She'd told him to call before he left his room, but she couldn't trust him to do that, and if she couldn't trust him, she couldn't do her job.

She stopped and scowled at the watercolor seascape above

the bed. Master Leong used to say that trust was like the sea. It could go out as fast as it came in.

Brenna had no idea what that meant. Never had. But the fact was, she was lying to herself. She didn't require trust to do her job. In fact, maybe she'd be more effective if she *didn't* trust him, if she was suspicious of everything and everybody. Glancing at the bedcover, she narrowed her eyes and made a decision.

BRENNA SQUIRMED. Her youngest brother twisted her arm more tightly behind her back. "Say uncle," he demanded in his pubescent voice.

But Brenna O'Shay never said uncle. She jerked forward...and awoke with a start.

It took her a moment to remember her circumstances, to realize she was scrunched up in a padded chair in a strange hotel room. She'd propped her door open with a phone book to allow herself an unobstructed view of Nathan's door.

Or it *would* be unobstructed if that man would get away from Fox's door.

Hey! There was a man by Nate's door! His hand was on the latch. The door was swinging open.

Brenna launched into the hall like a loose cannon. Mind foggy, eyesight blurry, legs unsteady, she slammed into the intruder's back, but managed to grab his arm, twist it upward, and yank him back into the hall.

"Hey!" he squawked.

"What are you doing here?" she growled, pushing his arm up higher.

"Let me go!"

He tried to wrench away. They scuffled sideways and bumped into the wall, but Brenna's adrenaline was pumping. She hung on like a bulldog.

"What are you doing here?" she rasped again.

"Let me go!" His voice was rising.

"Who gave you the key?"

"None of your business!" he cried. Spinning, he jerked his arm from her grasp and made his escape.

He didn't get twelve inches before she tackled him. He landed with a muffled grunt, her knees in the small of his back, and her grip already hard on his bent-up arm.

"Lie still and I won't hurt you."

He lay panting hard beneath her, but didn't try to struggle.

"I'll have some answers." Her own body was trembling, whether from excitement or fear, she wasn't certain. She could only hope he couldn't hear the quaver in her voice.

"O'Shay?" Nathan's voice startled her.

She jerked around to see him standing in the doorway, his eyes sleepy and his hair tousled.

"Get back inside!" she snapped.

"Okay," he acquiesced. "But...why are you sitting on Ian?"

She blinked. Adrenaline drained from her body like water down a drain. "Ian?"

Nathan nodded. "Ian. One of the road crew. He, uh..." Nate nodded toward the right to a pair of suitcases she hadn't noticed. "He brought up my luggage."

She squinted at the suitcases. Her stomach flipped over. "Oh."

Nathan nodded. "Maybe you should let him up."

She hesitated. How did she know what this man's intentions were? She took a long slow breath and remained where she was.

"Where'd you get the key, Ian?"

"Sarge gave it to me." His voice was muffled by the carpet and broke when he said it.

Poor Ian was neither very large nor very old, Brenna noticed suddenly. Guilt settled in. But, dammit, she'd been hired to do a job, and do it she would. If this man habitually brought up luggage in the wee hours of the morning, she sure as hell should have been informed.

"Why?"

"Sarge likes Nate to have it first thing in the morning. I just set it right inside his door. That's all."

"How long have you been in Mr. Fox's employ?"

"Huh?"

"How long have you been working for Fox?"

Brenna felt him tremble beneath her. "Two years going on."

"Oh." Brenna slipped off his back, feeling stupid as a drowning duck and refusing to admit it.

Ian rolled over and pushed his white-blond hair away from a face plagued by acne.

"Do you always bring up Mr. Fox's luggage, Ian?" she asked, still crouched beside him.

He nodded jerkily.

"Well, you won't be doing that anymore. From now on you bring the suitcases to me. I'll make sure Mr. Fox gets them."

"To you?" He shifted his gaze to Nathan as if for affirmation, but now was not the time to lose her edge. If she was going to gain the crew's respect she'd best start now.

"That's right. I've been hired to see to his security."

"But Sarge—"

"I'll talk to Sarge," she interrupted abruptly. "I'm sure he'll see things my way."

"I...I believe y'," Ian said, then scrambled to his feet and fled.

The hall went silent. Reaching forward, Brenna retrieved the card key from where Ian had dropped it. She rose more slowly.

Not surprisingly, Nathan's brows were somewhere in his hairline again. She made a valiant effort not to blush and reminded herself that she was here to protect him.

"So when were you going to tell me about *this,* Mr. Fox?"

He leaned up against the doorjamb. His gray sweatpants rode indecently low on his hips, his torso was bare, and she noticed without meaning to that there was a crescent-shaped scar in the center of his chest. She tried not to wonder how he'd gotten it. "Tell you what, Miss O'Shay?"

She gave him a peeved look and hoped it wasn't ruined by her blush. How was she supposed to know somebody delivered his luggage in the middle of the night? It was a stupid practice, stupid and dangerous. She had nothing to be embarrassed about.

"You agreed to call me before this door opened," she insisted.

"Did I?"

She narrowed her eyes at him. "Yes."

He grinned and caught her gaze with his own. "Then you're not very trusting, Miss O'Shay."

She stiffened her back. "What does that mean?"

He broke eye contact, shifting his gaze to the bedspread that had trailed into the hallway in her frantic lunge for Ian. "You were watching my door."

Her face felt warm, despite knowing she had nothing to be ashamed of. "I was merely trying to keep you safe from any potential threats."

"Or maybe you thought I would try to sneak out without telling you."

She pursed her lips. That was exactly what she thought, but there seemed little reason to admit it. "And why would you do that, Mr. Fox?"

The smile slipped slowly from his face. Even his eyes became somber. "Maybe because I don't want to be followed around like a damned winged grouse," he said softly.

Her emotions were getting all muddled—guilt, empathy, frustration. "I didn't come begging for this job," she said, knowing better than to try to defend herself to him.

"Didn't you?" His eyes were deadly earnest, and too damned knowing.

She refused to look away, although if the truth be known, she could easily have begged if she had thought it would do her any good. "No," she said, "I only came for an interview."

His gaze skimmed from her face, down her body and back up to her eyes. "Why?" His tone was breathy with honest amazement, but she'd heard that kind of tone too often. It was always followed by sneers.

"Because it's my job," she said, her voice rising. "Because I'm damned good at it. Because—"

A door jerked open. "Y'all don't shut up out here I'm gonna call the cops," a man growled. Unshaven, he scowled aggressively. His pajama shirt barely covered the gut hanging over striped trousers.

"Sorry." Nate grinned apologetically, then turned back to Brenna. "Come back to bed, honey," he said, conjuring up an exaggerated Southern drawl. "You're disturbing the folks. I'll play the wild stallion and the cowgirl again if you really want to."

Her jaw dropped.

Nate's grin broadened. "Come on."

Anger boiled up inside her. "You—"

"Now, now," he tsked, stepping into the hall to gently draw her forward. "How would it look if you got us in trouble for disturbing the peace...*again?*"

She wanted to give him a good solid knuckle punch to his ridiculously square jaw. But she'd just jumped poor Ian, and hotel security might not find a second attack really amusing, so she allowed herself to be drawn inside.

"Sorry," Nate said again, peeking around her at the pajama man. "Sleep tight." He turned away, then changed his mind. "Oh, if you hear any whinnying, just ignore it."

Stepping back, he let the door swing shut, pitching them into absolute darkness.

"So," his tone was low and amused. "Big night?"

She snorted, then reached for the light switch. Unfortunately, he was in the way. The muscles in his abdomen felt hard as sculpted marble against her fingers.

"Why, *honeybunch!*" he said, using that infuriating borrowed drawl. "I hardly know you."

Brenna yanked her hand back, suddenly grateful for the darkness to cover her infuriating embarrassment. "What do you want?" she asked.

"What do *you* want?"

She wanted him behind bars for sexual harassment. Or did they give the death penalty for that? "Mr. Fox," she said, pleased that her voice sounded relatively normal. "I know you think yourself quite irresistible. But let me assure you, I have no interest whatsoever in that regard."

"I'm so relieved," he drawled. "So why are you here?"

If she could just slap him once she would feel immensely better. "I'm here because you threatened me with hotel security," she said.

"I mean..." She could hear the grin in his voice. "Why are you guarding my body?"

"That's none of your business."

"Isn't it? I think I have a right to know a little something about my employees." He paused. All was silent. "Or should I call your agency?"

No! She almost screamed the word, but managed to remain quiet for a moment, stilling her panic. "It seems to me that if you had doubts about my abilities you should have voiced them *before* you hired me."

"I didn't say I doubted your ability."

"But you do," she said softly, and even now the realization hurt, but only because she had allowed herself to hope for a moment.

The room was silent again. Fox cleared his throat and shifted away slightly, perhaps to lean against the wall, though she couldn't tell for sure in the darkness. "Maybe I did doubt you," he said, "but that was before I saw you with your knee jammed into Ian's back."

There was laughter in his voice again. It should have irritated her. Instead, it seemed to soften the room somehow. But she could hardly afford to be softened.

"Are you saying you'll let me do my job then?" she asked.

He straightened abruptly and flipped the light on. Her eyes adjusted slowly, but when they did she was painfully aware of his state of undress. The darkness had seemed intimate, but somehow the light seemed even more so, for she could see every hard curve of his chest, every shadowed dip of his rippled abdomen.

"Do I look like the kind of man who needs a bodyguard?" he asked softly.

Sweet Mary! "No." The word came out a bit breathier than she had intended. "But what seems and what is can be as different as a caterpillar from a butterfly."

He was silent for a moment. "What the hell does that mean?"

She had no idea. "The fact is you *do* need a guard," she said, and turning, walked into the sitting room. Best to keep some space between them. His guitar was leaning against a wingback chair. She smoothed a finger along a single string and turned. "Appearances don't matter."

His gaze skimmed her. She hadn't changed her clothes from the day before, and felt wrinkled and gritty. But his expression suggested other things. "They do to me," he said softly.

She scowled and reminded herself to be offended. It didn't matter that his coffee-bean gaze made her feel warm all over. She was here for the job and nothing more. "Listen," she said, pleased by the gruff sound of her voice. "I've been hired to do a job and I'm going to do it."

"Goddamn it!" he swore, pacing up to glare down at her. "I need a bodyguard like I need a hole in my head!"

"And if you don't have a bodyguard you may very well *have* a hole in your head!" she snapped back.

He snorted. "You've been spending too much time with Sarge."

"You forget that I read the letters."

"Do you have any idea how many letters I get a month?"

"I don't see what that has to do with—"

"Hundreds."

"So?"

"Thousands a year. And out of them thousands I've got...what? Ten, maybe twelve letters that are even a shade off center. I think that's pretty safe odds."

"So you're saying you're not worried that ten or twelve guys have it in for you? You think you can handle them?"

He straightened to stare at her from his full height. "So tell me, little Miss Sashay, do you think you could do better? You think you could hold twelve guys off me?"

She lifted her chin slightly. Perhaps a roundhouse kick to the chops would make him more polite, but it probably would do nothing for her state of employment, contract or no contract. So she shrugged and turned away. "It doesn't matter, Mr. Fox."

"Doesn't matter?"

"No," she said. "Because the letters were all sent by the same person."

4

NATHAN STARED AT HER. He tried to appear nonchalant—the superstar in control, clever, bored even. But at his best he was, generally speaking, none of those things. And this was definitely not his best, with his mind fuzzy from lack of sleep and little sports socks encasing his teeth. But that wasn't the worst of it. He didn't like to talk about the letters. Not with anyone, and certainly not with someone who made his brain go numb and his groin go hard. Because, despite what he said, the letters gave him the creeps—made him feel vulnerable, as if he were being watched by malevolent eyes.

"What do you mean they're all written by the same person?" he asked, although he tried not to.

She shrugged, looking cool as a cucumber in her lime-green T-shirt and white cotton pants. Had she not slept at all, or did she always awaken this alert? Either option made him feel crotchety and irritable. Ten years ago he could play bars all night and work the ranch all day. But ten years ago he had been, well...ten years younger. No one could fault *his* logic.

"Just what I said," she answered. "They're all written by the same person."

"And what made you deduce that?" He crossed his arms against his chest and hoped he looked cynical instead of merely disheveled and foolish—and strangely chilled. He wasn't sure whether it was his shirtless state or talk of the letters that made him cold, but he was shivering. He hoped she didn't notice his spasmodic shaking. He'd already used his best irresistible stud act on her and she had been patently unimpressed. If the truth be told, neither her disinterest nor talk of the letters was doing a bit of good for his flagging self-esteem. Dammit! He dropped into a mauve upholstered chair and worked on his casual look. "The police never said anything about the letters being from the same guy."

"Maybe the police haven't had my experience."

Experience? She didn't look a day older than his favorite Stetson. "So you've been around?" he asked, letting the innuendo lie between them like Pandora's box.

She didn't open it, but scowled as she worked things out in her own mind. "Enough to know I'm right," she drawled confidently.

"That's crazy. None of the letters look even vaguely alike."

"That's one of the things that made me realize the truth." Though she acted nonchalant, he could hear the edge of excitement in her tone. "They're too different, as if they were intentionally made to *seem* different."

"A little amateur psychology, Miss O'Shay?" Her excitement intrigued him, but he knew enough of her kind to realize he'd be a fool to get involved. Despite her sweeter-than-honey looks, she was a climber, intent on getting to the top of her field no matter the cost to the others. He knew that. In fact, he bore the heel prints to prove it. "I didn't peg you as the therapist type. Thought you were more of the jump on their backs and bring out the rubber hose kind of girl."

"Afraid to admit I'm right, Mr. Fox?"

He snorted derisively, but suddenly he wasn't sure. There had always been something about those letters that had felt odd—besides the fact that they were mildly threatening. Which was pretty damn odd in itself if you thought about it, because he'd never hurt a soul in his life. Not intentionally anyway. Even in a dog-eat-dog world like the entertainment business, he'd been careful to step on no toes. Sarge, on the other hand, had ticked off more people than he could count, but was *he* the one getting ugly mail? No sirree. "They're from different people," he said, knowing he did so just to be contrary.

"You know that?" she asked, her sassy, strawberry mouth

quirking slightly. "Or are you thinking murderers are too honest to use aliases?" Her lips were very full. Watching them move mesmerized him somehow. "'Cause I gotta tell you, Fox, most murderers aren't always real up-front about everything."

Nathan brought his mind back to the business at hand. "That's crazy," he repeated. "Nobody said anything about murder. Nobody but you and Sarge anyhow, and each letter is different. The handwriting. Everything. Hell, some are typed. Some don't have signatures. Some talk like the guy's never even met me, and some—"

"Sounds like you've studied them pretty close for a man who's unconcerned about them."

Nathan rose abruptly to his feet and turned away. Oh yes, he'd studied them. Lots of other musicians had employees go through their mail for them, but he'd always loved that part, almost as much as being face to face with his fans. It irked him no end that those damned letters had put a pall over it. Each time he opened an envelope now, he wondered if it would be the proverbial bad apple. But he wasn't going to let it spook him. "I've read them," he said, settling his hip against the arm of the sofa.

"And they don't worry you?"

Their gazes met. For a moment he was tempted to tell her the truth. But dammit, what kind of man would admit that to someone with...breasts. And hers were such nice breasts. Just the sight of them made him fidgety...and irritable, because he was pretty damn sure that there was nothing on his body that made *her* fidget.

"If they worried me, would I have hired a guard who's smaller than my damn boot?" he snapped.

She stiffened. Now he'd gotten her riled. But dammit, he wasn't all that happy himself.

"You think I can't do the job."

"Listen. I hired you." To tell the truth, he was tired and frustrated and just damned mad. All he'd wanted was to make music—that was all. He didn't need the stardom. Yeah, the money was nice, but the schedule got wearing. Only the love of the fans never dulled, but now even that had a shadow over it. "I said I'd pay you good money and I ain't backing out. Just..." He spread a hand in front of him, feeling oddly desperate. It wasn't like him to feel cornered. "Don't crowd me."

"And by crowding you, you mean, don't do my job."

"All I'm asking you to do is keep Sarge happy and stay out of my way."

"That's going to be hard to do while I'm guarding you."

He straightened away from the sofa. "I can take care of myself."

She stepped up to him, eyes narrowed like an angry cat's. "No, you can't. Someone's out to get you and they mean business."

"Well, I sure ain't going to be hiding behind some little girl so she can prove she's got—"

"Little girl! Listen—"

"I'm giving you the best of everything. Lots of money and no work."

"Maybe I want the work."

He stared at her. Her eyes looked enormous in her flushed face, and her breathing seemed to match his own. "Why?" he asked.

"Because that's what I do."

There was such intensity, such need in her voice that he was almost sucked into her emotions, but he drew himself carefully back. "Not with me, you don't," he said softly.

"That's too bad." She blew out a breath, her hands balled into fists as she stepped back a pace. "Your fans will be disappointed."

"What?"

"When I sue you for sexual harassment. When I tell the reporters that I signed on in good faith only to find out you're a groping lech."

He tightened his fists, letting the anger boil in him, but keeping his tone level. "I haven't groped..." He let the corner of his lips curl and remained where he was, though he wanted nothing more than to give her a good shaking. "Yet."

"Nathan Fox is a legend," she said in that sweet Southern drawl. "An all-round good guy. I'm sure the paparazzi will be interested in whatever I have to tell them."

"Blackmail?" he asked, his voice marvelously even.

Her eyes hardened even further, though he wouldn't have thought it possible. "I just want to do my job without any interference from you. I don't think that's too much to ask."

In the stillness, it seemed he could hear the thrum of his own pulse. "You just want to be one of the guys?" he asked.

"That's right." Her tone was stern, her small face somber. "Just one of the guys."

"You don't have the balls for it."

"Try me," she said, and turning, left the room.

ON FRIDAY, BRENNA WATCHED the road crew set up the stage, oversaw Nathan's interview, took notes on a thousand minute details, and finally saw The Fox safely to his hotel room.

That night, dressed in panties and an oversized T-shirt she'd inherited from a brother, she sat cross-legged on her bed and went through more mail. There were hundreds of letters from all over the world. The majority of them were from women—a lot of gushers, a few marriage proposals, and a couple of really pathetic cases offering to bear his child.

It was long past midnight when she came across a letter that struck a familiar and disconcerting note in her sleep-fogged brain. Brenna shoved her gold-rimmed glasses farther up her nose and read it again. It was handwritten on pink stationery with a kitten at the top. The beginning read like most of the others, praising Nate's musical talents and sexy good looks. It was just a couple of lines near the close that seemed out of place. Just a couple of lines, but it was enough.

"Take care of yourself, Nathan. Make sure you eat right. A heart attack can be just as fatal as a bullet."

What kind of woman would say that in a fan letter? And

why? Did she know about Nathan's eating habits? And if so, how? In all the articles Brenna had read, she'd never heard any mention of his love of food—everything else, but not that.

Brenna read the letter again, then again. It was signed Angela and postmarked Eureka, Nevada, but there was no return address. That, too, was strange. Surely a fan wouldn't discourage any kind of return mail from her hero.

Tossing the letter aside, Brenna rose and stretched, her body tense and her mind buzzing. She needed to take better care of herself, but how could she do that when she spent the whole day dogging an overcharged superstar who exuded sex appeal and raw humor with mind-numbing regularity? Her first day of following him around had explained his lack of fat.

Circling her small sitting area, Brenna rolled her shoulders and tried not to think of how he had looked while talking to the latest batch of reporters. He'd dressed in nothing more shocking than a pair of black jeans, a chamois-colored corduroy shirt, and his huge, signature belt buckle. He'd left his hat behind and his eyes had sparkled with that deadly kind of mischief that would inspire the reporters to compare his eyes to something ridiculous, like maple syrup.

But they had not looked syrupy when they turned on her. No. For her, they registered flat rejection, as if she weren't even there, even though she'd never been more than three steps behind him all day.

There was no more of that teasing innuendo, that nerve-tingling closeness. Just one of the guys, he'd said, but it was obvious she was less than that. And it was a good thing too, Brenna reminded herself quickly.

He was her boss. And not only that, he was a chauvinistic boss with no more faith in her abilities than her own family had. She was here to prove him wrong, to prove them all wrong. To find out who was sending the letters, to stop the threats, to solve the mystery. And the key lay in the letters.

Turning wearily, Brenna retrieved another bag of mail and hauled it onto her bed.

"HEY, O'SHAY. YOU AWAKE?"

Brenna opened her eyes. Blank white made up her first view of the morning.

"Hey. Wake up."

A minute ago the voice had come from the hall. But now it sounded from beside her bed. Brenna sat up with a start, a letter stuck to her cheek as she scrambled for a blanket. But she'd never burrowed under the covers. The paper that had been stuck to her cheek, fell away.

"Hey." Nathan grinned down at her. "You ready to go?"

"What the hell are you doing in my room?" she rasped, trying to pull the worn T-shirt down over her knees.

"I have keys to all you guys' rooms. We're always getting our stuff mixed up. Makes life easier if we can just jump in there and dig it out."

She moved her lips, trying to put words to why he couldn't be here, but everything was foggy and dim, including her eyesight. Where had she put her glasses?

"Come on. Gotta get a wiggle on. We're burning daylight," he said.

"You…" She glanced frantically about. Did she have a robe? Pants? What kind of panties had she worn, and were they visible from his vantage point? "You're supposed to call me before you leave your room."

"Yeah, well…" He sat down on the bed and casually pushed her bare feet aside. "My door was all of two yards from yours. I thought I could risk it.

"You got a little—" he motioned toward her cheek "—a little drool there."

Brenna smacked her hand to the side of her face. The lines etched in her cheek by the letter were deep enough to plant turnip seeds. Sweet Mary! And here he was looking like something from a cowboy calendar, dressed in his usual jeans and white T-shirt.

"What are you doing here?" she asked. Her voice had all the charm of a cantankerous bullfrog.

"Time to go running. I knew you'd be madder than a bear

cat if I went without you. But you'd best hurry and get ready
before I'm out of the mood.''

She felt her jaw drop. What mood? Their gazes met.

He grinned. "For running." He slapped her leg as if they
were old buddies. "Come on, O'Shay. Get your mind out of
the gutter." He stood quickly and lifted yesterday's slacks
from a nearby chair. "You gotta have something better than
this." He turned toward her suitcase, which had been cau-
tiously left outside her door the previous night. "Sweats in
here?" he asked, and flipped her case open.

"I…" she began, but he was already rummaging through
her underwear to her clothes underneath.

"Now we're talking," he said, pulled out a pair of gray,
drawstring shorts, and tossed them to her. "Get dressed."

"Get out!" She motioned vaguely toward the door. The
words were a bit more high-pitched than she'd intended.

"And risk life and limb to any passerby?" he asked.
"What if I get snuffed out? How would that look on your
record? Come on now. Get in them shorts. You need a bra?"

Her eyes popped. His dropped to her chest.

"Yep. You do." He turned away to rummage about in her
luggage again.

For a moment she was beyond thought, but sitting here in
her underwear didn't seem like the best of options, so she
slipped into her shorts and pulled the drawstring sloppily
tight. She considered shoving her glasses on, then decided
against it and hated herself for doing so.

"This it?" he asked, holding Victoria's best secret in one
hand. "Wow!" He examined it from close proximity, fin-
gering the black lace and the thick underpadding. "You
could use that for a body shield if you're ever in a shoot-out
huh? I really don't think you need the extra—"

"Give me that!" She rose with a start and snatched it from
his fingers.

"You're kind of touchy for one of the guys. And pretty
messy. You always like this?" he asked, sweeping his hand
over the pile of loose letters.

"I was busy reading," she said, and headed for the bathroom, but in a moment, she realized her mistake. Tromping back to her suitcase, she dropped the lacy article he'd retrieved and snatched up a sports bra.

"Yeah?" He watched her head back toward the bathroom. "How many marriage proposals were there?"

She slammed the door shut behind her. Nathan let his shoulders droop. Geez! Being around this woman was more likely to kill him than save him. First, he'd tried to act as if she were one of the guys. That had been a patent failure. So then he had attempted to pretend she simply didn't exist. But it wasn't in his character to ignore someone who had...well...breasts, and certainly not anyone like *her*.

The truth had been painfully obvious. He couldn't ignore her or treat her like one of the guys. The guys didn't have legs like that. And the upper body thing! Geez! He paced around the corner of her bed. He was acting like a sex-crazed teenager. But there was just something about this woman. Okay, yeah, there was no shortage of women who were interested in him. But life on the road wasn't exactly the wild orgy people thought it was. Early in his career he had been rather overwhelmed by his female fans' adoration, and perhaps he'd done a few things he shouldn't have, especially after Shauna Summers dumped him to move up the musical ladder. But he'd learned soon enough that that kind of no-strings-attached relationship wasn't for him.

He was just a farm boy from North Dakota, and if his mom thought he was playing fast and loose with the women, she'd march down here and box his ears.

The truth was, he no longer knew how to treat women, because he only met two types these days. There was the Shauna Summers type with all the ambition of a bulldozer and the emotional tenderness to match, and there was the type that saw him as some sort of traveling stud. In the end, he'd found it safest to simply concentrate on his music. To enjoy the good parts, get through the bad, and return each year to Five Crow Farm, his thousand-acre haven in the North.

He wished, in fact, that he were there now. Suddenly he

felt decidedly melancholy. Turning toward the bed, he scowled at the letters. Even now they made his stomach feel vaguely sick, but dammit, he wasn't going to let one harebrained lunatic get to him. He scowled at the thought. Two days ago he would have said he wasn't going to let a dozen harebrained lunatics get to him.

He turned brusquely toward the bathroom door, determined to improve his mood. And how better to do that than to harass a beautiful woman?

"Hey, O'Shay, what you doing in there?"

She didn't answer. The thought that she might be as uncomfortable with the situation as he was brightened his mood considerably. So he knocked on the door with two knuckles. "I'm not going to have to come in there and make sure you're all right, am I?"

He heard the water turn off just before the door opened with a jerk. "Has anyone ever told y' you're extraordinarily irritating?"

He drew back as if startled. "No, mostly they tell me I'm just a damned nice guy," he said. He couldn't help but grin, because she was the cutest little security guard he'd ever seen, what with her face fresh-scrubbed and her hair pulled back in a crinkled ponytail. He leaned close. She smelled like apricots. "You sure you're thinking of the right fella?"

"Absolutely," she said. Even her grouchy tone tickled him.

"It's not too late to quit," he said, "or be promoted."

She raised one red eyebrow at him. "To what?"

He shoved his hands into his back pockets, hoping he looked boyish, and hoping even more that she wouldn't slap him silly. "Who knows?" he said. "Make me a suggestion."

Her full lips pursed and her brows scrunched over snapping green eyes. "I suggest you get out on the road, Fox, before I make good on my threat and slap you with sexual harassment."

He grinned as he turned toward the door. "Slap me with anything you want, honey. Just tell me what position to assume."

"Sweet Mary," she murmured, and he laughed as they jogged down the hall and stopped at his room for him to change clothes.

It was a full hour later when they returned to their rooms. Sweaty, tired and sore, Brenna felt as if she'd been greased like a pig and whipped like a cur. For a man who confessed to being lazy, Nathan ran like a Thoroughbred.

"Tired?" he asked, leaning against his doorjamb as she slipped in the key card.

She shifted her gaze up to his. "You?"

He laughed. The sound seemed to come from somewhere deep inside his chest, and despite the tension between them, it made her insides go all gushy and her toes curl inside her sneakers.

"Not unless you are," he said.

She stepped inside and he followed.

"Are you always this insecure, Fox?" she asked, glancing about the room before slipping into the next to make sure it was safe.

"Are you?" he asked.

She raised her brows in question.

He motioned toward her as she approached him again. "You planning on doing this every time I walk into a room?"

"Until I figure out who's out to get you."

"Will you quit sounding like Cagney?"

Despite herself, she couldn't help but feel silly under his amused stare. And although the run had awakened her, comparing her disheveled state to his perfection for half an hour on the road hadn't exactly put her spirits in peak form. "Maybe it's time you start taking the threats more seriously, Fox."

"I don't think I could look as gloomy as you if I tried."

"I do not look gloomy. I look professional."

He laughed. "If you look that glum during rehearsal, there'll be hell to pay. Paul's as sensitive as a schoolgirl. If he looks up and sees you scowling like that he's likely to think his timing's off and burst into tears."

"Rehearsal?"

He raised his brows. "In half an hour."

"Half an hour?" She put her hand self-consciously to her hair, and he laughed, seeming to read her thoughts.

"Better get a wiggle on, honey. Who knows what evil might befall me during rehearsal."

Brenna considered a half-dozen stinging rejoinders. But there was no time for any of them. Because she'd rather take a slug for him than look like a drowned ferret while he crooned out love songs to an imaginary audience.

THE REHEARSAL WAS MORE INFORMAL than Brenna had expected. She watched him as he hummed a couple of bars into the microphone, then she stopped a security guard as he passed by. Nathan and The Cowboys performed tonight, giving her very little time to prepare for the crowds.

But the security guard was none too helpful. He wasn't certain how many men were assigned for that night's performance, but managed to produce a map of the coliseum.

From up on stage, Brenna heard Nate make a couple of suggestions about lighting. She turned her attention back to the map, figuring how many guards she'd need front stage, back stage, near the exit.

"You coming?" Nathan asked, passing her at high speed, boots ringing on the concrete floor.

"Where you going?" She glanced up, mouth ajar. But he didn't stop, giving her no choice but to hurry after him. She felt ridiculously like a snot-nosed kid chasing her big brother as she trotted along in his wake.

"Radio station. Got a car waiting."

"I thought you had to rehearse."

"I did."

The *car* was a stretch limousine. The driver opened the back door and Nate motioned her inside before him. For a moment she considered reminding him that she was not his date. But this hardly seemed the time, so she slipped onto the white leather seats. He slid in beside her.

In a moment, they were on their way. The upholstery was

soft and cushy, the movement relaxing, making her realize how tired she was. She slumped a little deeper into the cushions. Nathan laid his arm across the back of the seat and stretched his half-mile legs out in front of him.

"Pretty cozy, huh?" he said, grinning down at her. "Kind of romantic?"

She sat up with a start. She should have known better than to relax around him. "I'll need to have a copy of your agenda from now on."

"Agenda?"

"Yeah. Your interviews, rehearsals, social functions…"

"Social functions? Are you saying you want me to check it out with you before I go on a date?"

She averted her gaze and glanced down at the map still in her hand. "I'm saying I need to be informed. And I'll need a dossier on anyone you're meeting with."

She could feel his gaze on her face.

"Tell me, O'Shay, are you just trying to make my life hell for kicks or do you have ulterior motives?"

She lifted her gaze, and immediately wished she hadn't, for once again the line about maple syrup eyes came to mind. How sappy was that! She raised her chin a notch. "Ulterior motives?"

"Maybe you're just trying to make my social life so difficult that I won't have any choice but to date *you*."

"And maybe there's not room for me in this car," she said, keeping her voice Southern-sweet. "What with your ego and all."

He stared at her for a moment and then laughed. "The great thing about you, O'Shay, is that you make them threat letters seem like a breath of fresh air," he said, and turning toward the window, chuckled to himself.

5

BRENNA CHECKED HERSELF IN THE MIRROR. It was nearly time to leave the hotel for the auditorium. Nearly time for her most crucial test. She'd met with the usual security guards, discussed a hundred details with Sarge, and memorized the layout of the auditorium.

Now, dressed in a sleeveless ivory jumpsuit with a short, matching jacket, she looked professional enough, while still not resembling a pit bull. She hoped. Brenna bit her lip, wondering if she'd gone too far with her hair. She'd pinned it up at the back of her head. But it had looked harsh and old-fashioned, so she'd pulled a few tendrils loose and let them fall down beside her ears. It had only taken a few minutes. Still, she felt somewhat guilty, as if looking good was somehow at odds with her profession. But Fox had made it very clear that he had no desire to be followed around by a trained mastiff.

So surely a spritz of perfume wouldn't hurt.

She reached for the bottle and dispensed the spray without allowing another fretful thought, then hurried toward the door.

But his knock came before she reached it.

"Hey, O'Shay, you—"

She jerked it open. "You're supposed to call me before you leave your room!"

His mouth fell open.

"Geez, O'Shay, you look really...not like one of the guys."

She was not going to blush, she told herself, and cleared her throat. "Call me next time."

He dropped a shoulder against the doorjamb. "Why?"

"Listen, Fox, I'm not your date. I'm your bodyguard."

He leaned closer, looking hopelessly boyish, with his hat in his hand and his bone-colored shirt buttoned to the collar. "Can't you be both?" he asked.

She opened her mouth to object, but he laughed and motioned her forward.

"Car's waiting."

The trip from the hotel to the auditorium was quick and without incident. The band talked amongst themselves, allowing Brenna to contact her counterparts by the headset which was wired to her belt.

At their destination, Brenna stepped out first, made certain the path to the auditorium was clear and safe, and allowed Nate and his band to hurry inside.

After that, the evening rushed by as if on wheels. Brenna scurried from one place to the next, watching the crowd, making certain the band's entrance stayed clear, maintaining radio contact with the driver, Sarge, and the local guards.

The opening act wound up its performance. Brenna rushed backstage, knocked once, then spent an agonizing moment wondering if she should just pop inside. After all, it wasn't as if Fox had wasted any respect for *her* modesty. But before she had found a solution to the debate, the door opened and Nathan stepped out with the others behind him.

"Ready?" she asked, tense as a fiddle string and hyped as a racehorse.

Nathan, on the other hand, looked as calm as an eggplant. "For what?" he asked, leaning close.

"Your performance."

"Oh." He chuckled. "Yeah. You nervous?"

"No!" She said it too quickly.

"Good." Closer still. "Would you slap me for sexual harassment if I said you look great?"

"Probably not."

"How 'bout if I said you smell good enough to eat?"

"Over the line, Fox."

"How far over?" he asked.

"Get out of here," she said, and he laughed.

They trooped through the coliseum. Brenna saw them safely to the stage, listened to the applause roar up, then scurried around the front to watch the crowd. Everything seemed to be secure, in place, safe.

Brian Mueller started playing the fiddle. The crowd fell quiet, and then Nathan opened his performance with a rowdy drinking song that had the fans on their feet and singing along in minutes.

"Ms. O'Shay?" a voice shouted above the noise.

Brenna turned to find a hulking security guard addressing her. "Smitty, isn't it?"

"Yeah. I just wanted to double-check about them exit routes. You want more than one, right?"

"That's right. I don't want the whole band going out the same door."

"What's that?"

"I don't want—" she began, louder this time, then took the big man's arm and ushered him to a quieter spot where she could dispense instructions. A hundred details sped by before she could return inside.

By then the mood of the music had changed dramatically. Nathan stood center stage, his hat gone and the top two buttons of his shirt undone. Perspiration shone on his face and his hair gleamed in the harsh overhead lights. But it was his expression, both in his music and on his face, that drew the attention of every soul in the place. The song was a simple melody, a story set to music, conjuring up a thousand poignant images. It was the tale of a young boy who grew up alone. As a teenager, he never fit in. As a young man, his love was rejected.

Despite herself, Brenna felt the music fill her, felt the emotion build.

Nathan lifted one open hand before him, as if in supplication for love, and though Brenna called herself a thousand kinds of fool, she couldn't help being sucked in by the mood.

But suddenly a movement caught her attention. A woman was descending the aisle, hurrying toward the stage.

Brenna's carefully honed battle instincts rushed to the fore. She launched forward. But Smitty was already on the job. He apprehended the woman some twenty feet from the stage and bent to talk to her.

Brenna watched from close proximity as the woman turned back. Nathan sang on, his tone no less alluring. But suddenly, the woman turned, bolted past the hulking guard, and sprinted for the stage.

Without thought, without premeditation, Brenna sprang into action. She snagged the galloping woman just before she reached her destination.

"Let me go." The woman was, as they say in the movies, drunk and disorderly—a hard-faced gal with hair dyed blond and enough makeup to keep the trowel stock high.

"You'll have to take your seat," Brenna said, keeping a firm hold on her arm.

"Let go of me!" Her voice was rising.

Brenna dropped her arm. "Take your seat."

She staggered a little. "I just want to give him my phone number."

"I'll tell you what, give it to me, and I'll make sure he gets it."

The woman looked her over, then snorted. "Right," she said and tried to shove Brenna aside.

Brenna swept her arms away with a side block, then reached in, grabbed her by one wrist and forced it up behind her back. "Get your butt in a seat," she growled, "or I'll have it thrown out of here faster than it takes your makeup to gel."

"Sorry about that," rumbled Smitty from beside her.

"Not your fault," Brenna assured him. "See her to her seat. And make sure you get her phone number to give to Mr. Fox."

"Yes, ma'am," he said.

Brenna dropped her arm, then skimmed the crowd again as Smitty escorted their runaway back up the aisle.

All seemed well, so Brenna went up the stairs and out of sight from the hundreds of people that packed the seats.

Sweet Mary, she felt as if her heart was going to leap out of her chest, and her hands were shaking like wind chimes in a hurricane.

But what a rush!

"What are you doing here?" someone asked from behind.

Brenna spun toward the voice. And there, not ten feet away, stood her youngest brother.

"Brady!"

"Don't you 'Brady' me. We've been worried sick 'bout you." He wore that tough-guy expression he used to use when they played commandos together. It brought back a hundred aged memories, and with them, a rush of vintage guilt.

"What are you doing—running off without so much as a goodbye? We thought you'd up and got yourself murdered or something."

"I sent Shamus a letter," Brenna said and glanced nervously toward the doorway to the auditorium, hoping no one would see this encounter.

"Yeah. And you said you were going to be some singer's traveling secretary. Not a damned bodyguard! What were you thinking—lying to Bartman and everything?"

She felt herself pale. "You didn't tell him, did you?"

"I probably should have. But he's sure to figure it out for himself. Someone called him just the other day. Asked if they had a guard named O'Shay."

"Someone called?" Her knees felt weak. "Who?"

"How the hell would I know?"

"Was it Fox? No! It couldn't have been. Was it a man? What kind of voice? Did he—"

"Dammit, Brenna! I just came to bring you home."

She straightened. "How did you find me?"

"I'm a cop, Brenna. You think I can't track down my own sister?"

In fact, she'd known they would find her eventually. But she'd thought that by then she would have proven her ability. "Well." She shrugged, but she couldn't help feeling that she was five again, even with her *youngest* brother. "You found me. So you go on home and tell everyone I'm fine."

He snorted again. "Not without you, I'm not. Shamus said to bring you home."

"You told Shamus where I was?" Oh, no! It was bad enough having Brady here. But Shamus was the oldest of the six of them, and had always been the undisputed ringleader of the commando squad. It was he, in fact, who decided Brenna could no longer be a cop once their mother died. After that, she'd been lucky to be one of the robbers. Though, if the truth be known, she'd made a damn fine thief.

"'Course I told Shamus," Brady said. "You think we was just going to let you get yourself killed somewhere?"

"I'm not going to…" One of the security guards passed by. She straightened her back and lowered her voice. "I'm not going to get myself killed, and I'm not seven years old, Brady. I'm twenty-three. Old enough to make my own decisions."

"So you decided to be a *bodyguard?* Brenna! What are you thinking?"

"I'm thinking I've got a job to do and I'm damn good at it. So you hike on back to Poplar Springs and call off the hounds," she said, and pivoted away, heart thumping and nerves jamming.

But she didn't get fifteen feet down the aisle before Brady caught her arm. "This is crazy, Brenna."

She yanked her arm from his grasp. "What's crazy is that you can't let me live my own life."

"Shamus said to bring you home, so I'm bringing you home," he said, and pulled her close.

"What do you think you're doing, bub?" asked Smitty from her immediate right.

"I'm not looking for any trouble," Brady said. "I'm just having a conversation with my—"

"Take your hands off her and back away."

"Listen," Brady began. "I'm a—"

"Get out of here now and I won't cause you any trouble,"

Brenna whispered. "But keep this up and I swear you'll regret it."

"I've got to do it," he said. "Come on."

He gave her arm a tug, but training and adrenaline made it simple to break free. Brady stepped in close, and she gave him a light knuckle punch to the belly. He doubled over in surprise, and in that second she reached around quick as light. Snatching his wallet from his back pocket, she stashed it up her sleeve.

Smitty was staring openmouthed at the doubled-over man. When he turned his gaze to Brenna, his eyes were wide with either admiration or shock, she wasn't sure which.

"Do you want me to turn him over to the police, ma'am?"

She didn't hesitate for a moment. "I think you'd better, Smitty. I told him twice he couldn't bring alcoholic beverages in here. I guess he took it personally."

"Had a little too much to drink, buddy?" Smitty asked, taking hold of Brady's arm.

"Brenna!" Brady warned.

"I think he's delusionary," Brenna said. "He seems to think he knows me. Better let him sleep it off in jail."

"I'm a police officer," Brady gritted, straightening slowly and glaring at his sister.

"Sure y' are," Smitty said.

"My badge is in my wallet." With his free hand, he slapped his back pocket. It was empty.

Brenna swallowed and stepped back a pace.

"Brenna!" Brady snarled, realizing she'd resurrected her old character from their childhood and was once again playing the thief.

"Come on," Smitty urged.

"She took my ID."

"'Course she did," Smitty said, pushing Brady up the aisle in front of him.

"Let me go!" Brady snarled. He tried to twist away, but Smitty wasn't about to be out-maneuvered a second time. Grabbing an arm, he shoved his prisoner up the aisle and out of sight.

"O'SHAY?"

Brenna didn't have time to answer before her room door was shoved open.

"You decent?" Nathan asked, peeking inside.

"Would it matter?" she asked wearily.

"Oh yeah." He chuckled as he stepped inside and looked her over. "You've got glasses."

She tried not to shuffle her feet as she pushed the wire rims up her nose.

"Cute. What happened to the T-shirt thing?"

She managed a scowl. "Just trying to be one of the guys." She wore full pajamas, a couple sizes too large, dark green, and buttoned to the chin. She'd slipped into them as soon as she'd returned to her room, because it had been one hell of a long night. Still, she consoled herself with the fact that she'd lived through her first performance, had only been attacked twice and had her little brother incarcerated.

God help her!

"That's not what the guys wear. Least it's not what *I* wear," Nate said.

Brenna stared at him in the ensuing silence. He looked cuddly and a little sleepy, and suddenly she wished, for her own self-preservation, that her pajamas had more buttons to fasten.

"Aren't you going to ask?" he said.

"I don't want to know what you wear," she lied.

He laughed aloud, walked with his hundred-acre stride across her sitting room and collapsed into the nearest chair. "So what did you think?"

She thought that if he were any more alluring she could use him for bait. And truthfully, she would have loved to curl up in his lap and tell him that her big brothers were going to be really, really mad at her, and she'd been scared to death, but in a kind of exhilarated way, and his singing was so pretty, it had almost made her cry. And... "What do I think about what?" she asked, trying to sound casual in the harsh face of carnal lust and more.

"About the concert," he said.

She shrugged, wishing she could conjure up a yawn. "I don't know much about country music."

"Okay." His smile didn't dim. "How about music in general?"

"Did you come in here to fish for compliments, Fox?"

"I've always liked to fish," he said, then released a long breath and settled back a mite, stretching his booted feet out in front of him. "Actually, I came to thank you."

"What?"

"For keeping the peace. I saw the woman by the stage." He paused. "And later, I saw you tussle with that fellow up top."

She felt the blush starting at her toes. He'd witnessed her fight with Brady. Damn! What if he decided to investigate and found out she'd had her own brother thrown in jail? That wouldn't look so good. "You did?"

"Yeah. Sometimes those drunks can be real bastards. You okay?"

"Uh, yeah. Sure."

"One of the security guards told Sarge I should pay you more. Said you're a real scrapper."

She tried not to fidget and made an attempt at changing the subject. "I don't think I was what Sarge had in mind when he was looking for a bodyguard."

"But you were just what I was looking for. Sarge should have known that."

Yes, he probably should have. It was just like Nathan Fox to hire the most feminine bodyguard in the room. And that had been her hands down. "I think he resents me." It sounded moodier than she had intended, and far too honest.

"Naw," Nathan said, his tone smoky soft. "He's just not used to seeing a woman do stuff he can't. They said it was really something how you handled that guy."

"He was, um…" She cleared her throat and turned away to fuss with the jacket she'd hung over her bedpost. "The guy was real drunk. Not much of a threat."

"That's not what I heard. They said he had a gun."

Sweet Mary! Carrying concealed! Of course he was.

Brenna knew Brady would be in trouble without his ID, had even hoped he'd be in enough trouble to hold him for a while. But in that fraction of a second when she'd snatched her brother's wallet, she'd never thought of his gun. She'd already put his billfold in the mail along with an apology in the belief that Brady would be home in a day or so. But…carrying concealed! Even she'd known enough to leave her Glock in Mississippi.

"I'm sure he didn't mean any real harm," she said weakly.

"I don't know," Nate said. "Could be this is the guy that's been sending the letters."

Brenna just about thumped her head against the wall, but could hardly admit the truth of the situation. "I'll…um, I'll keep tabs on what the police find out."

"I know."

"What?"

"I'm starting to think you're a real bodyguard."

She swung toward him on her bare heel. "What did you think I was?"

He rose to his feet. His warm gaze skimmed her body with breath-stopping intimacy. "I thought you were a woman with really great…coordination."

She raised one brow at him.

He grinned. "The way you fell into my arms that first day in the restaurant, I thought…how many gals could do that so nice on the first try?"

"I'm glad you appreciate my feeble attempts to please you," she retorted.

His grin widened. "Oh, I do. But since then I've figured out there's more to you."

"Dare I hope?"

"Yep. You got really nice hair too."

She watched him with arch curiosity for a moment. "You know, Fox, I can never decide if I should hit you in the gut or just file that complaint."

"Sexual harassment again?"

"Good guess."

"I've always been confused about this harassment thing.

Often as not, I can't tell it from your run-of-the-mill compliment. Seems I can't say anything to you.''

"Not true, Fox," she said, turning away. "You could talk about anything from the weather to the price of tea.''

"You know, the weather down here ain't hardly worth mentioning. If there ain't icicles hanging off body parts, I'm pretty much bored with the climate. And tea ain't my drink of choice. So that leaves me with—'' his gaze skimmed her again "—more interesting stuff.''

"Watch yourself," she warned, but her body had begun to thrum evilly.

He grinned. "Tell you what, O'Shay, if you'll allow just a couple lewd remarks, I'll let you harass the hell outta me.''

"How generous.''

"I know. But I mean it. Any time you feel like commenting on any of my parts, you go right ahead.''

"I'm honored.''

"Yeah? Where do you want to start?''

She tried not to smile, but he looked so ridiculously sincere. "I'm really surprised you're allowed to roam the streets free, Fox.''

"And I'm surprised you hide away a smile like that," he said, stepping up close.

She swiped the dastardly expression from her face and shook her head. "I'll walk you back to your room," she said, and skirted him to head for the door.

"So the boogeyman doesn't get me?" he asked, following her into the hall.

"So I can get some sleep without knocking you on the head.''

"Maybe you'd better check under my bed again.''

"Listen, Fox," she said, inserting the key, "if you're so desperate for companionship, I got a phone number from the woman at the auditorium.''

"The one you wrestled back to her seat?''

"The same.''

He winced as he stepped into his room. "Generally speaking, I prefer women who don't rush me while I'm working.''

"Really? I'm surprised at your integrity."

"You might be surprised by a lot of things about me."

"I doubt it."

"Wanna bet?"

From the corner of her eye, Brenna caught a glimpse of Ian's towhead, but before she could turn and apologize for the other night, he had disappeared around the corner, apparently hotfooting it in the opposite direction.

"Huh?" she said, scowling at Ian's fidgety nature. True, she'd jumped on his back and interrogated him in the wee hours of the morning, but that was no reason to be so skittish.

"Come on in," Nathan said. "I'll shock your socks off."

"Sorry. Not wearing any."

"Underwear?"

"Fox!"

He laughed, then sobered and lifted her hand from his door latch to his lips.

Feelings as bright as a meteor shower sparked through her as the breath was sucked from her lungs.

"Good night, O'Shay. You're a hell of a woman," he said, and let the door close behind him.

6

THEY LAID OVER IN CHARLOTTE for three days, giving Brenna a chance to study The Cowboys' upcoming agenda, contact future performance sites, and take care of a hundred other details.

Everyone seemed rested and relaxed when they packed back into the buses and headed toward Mena, a town on the western border of Arkansas that boasted just over five thousand people. Abner Days was Mena's big spring event, and the city had pooled its money to book The Cowboys as major entertainment.

Tennessee was rolling and green and beautiful, but Brenna ignored the scenery, dragged out another bag of mail, and pored over the contents as they traveled west.

Sometime after noon, the occupants of the buses could tolerate the confinement no longer. They stopped at a roadside park and had an impromptu picnic on blankets they dragged from the beds.

Although Brenna was insistent on working, the boys refused to allow it, and she was coerced out into the sunshine. The unusually warm weather had cooled a little and popcorn clouds dotted an azure sky. The sweet scents of dogwood and wisteria filled the air.

Conversation lulled and swelled around Brenna as she munched on crackers and cheese and tried not to be drawn into the boys' lives. They were like nothing more than a big, fractious family, and honestly, she had enough family troubles without borrowing someone else's.

"A plumber," Paul Grand was saying.

"No way!" Rover was not one to mince words.

"Your mom wanted you to be a plumber?" Fry said in amazement. "She musta not liked you much either, huh?"

"Good money in plumbing," Paul said, lying back, half on the blanket and half on the grass.

"Yeah," Fry said. "Enough to buy a bullet when you can't stand the excitement no more." Putting two fingers to his skull, he pulled an imaginary trigger.

Brenna couldn't help but chuckle with the others.

"How 'bout you, O'Shay?" Nathan's question sobered her abruptly.

"Me what?"

He raised his brows as if surprised by the tension in her tone. She was going to have to become accustomed to having him around, which seemed about as easy as living with a porcupine in your underwear.

"What did your mom want you to be?"

"Um. Momma died when I was twelve."

Nate grimaced. "Sorry."

She shrugged, hoping she managed to look nonchalant.

"Way to go, Fox," Fry murmured. "Ever want someone to bring down the mood, hire The Fox."

"You got to play to your talents," Nathan said, then turned back to Brenna. "How 'bout your dad?"

"Daddy died in the line of duty nearly three years ago."

"Dammit, Fox, we're leaving you out here for the squirrels to feed on," Fry said.

Nathan ignored him. "He was a police officer?"

"Sheriff."

"Did he want you to follow in his footsteps? Be one of Jackson's finest?"

Brenna opened her mouth to answer, but in that moment, panic seized her. Her father hadn't worked in Jackson; he'd worked in Poplar Springs, their hometown. But she dared not tell Fox, because that might only encourage more questions. He might find out she wasn't a bodyguard for Bartman at all, but a secretary with no experience, no backing, and no confidence in her ability to keep her mouth shut when Nathan was questioning her.

"I'd better get back to work," Brenna said, and jerked to her feet, nearly spilling the last of Nathan's milk before hurrying off to the bus.

More than an hour passed before Brenna was able to relax. She was going to have to get over this. Become a better actress, she told herself.

Sometime in the afternoon, Nathan ran out of milk. Fry jokingly worried about calcium withdrawal. Fox drank more milk than the combined population of most small states.

The convenience store where they stopped was a small, rundown establishment with two gas pumps and a cracked front window.

"Want me to go in for y', boss?" Atlas asked, turning from behind the steering wheel.

"No. I got to..." Nathan glanced at Brenna. She lifted her eyes, feeling his gaze on her. "Do some private business," he finished lamely.

"See how having a woman around improves us," Fry observed. "He was gonna say take a piss. But y'all know that'd be crude what with a lady around and all."

Brenna turned a wry expression to Fry. Though she still had trouble handling Nate's hot sensuality, she was becoming accustomed to the other men.

"Excuse me, gentlemen," she said, rising, "and I use that term ever so casually. I have a body to guard."

"Better lock the door, Fox. She's awful zealous," Fry said, and Brenna exited to their chuckles.

Oh, boy. It was like being caged up with a bunch of half-grown pups, she thought, but she couldn't quite help grinning as she entered the store.

Nathan went straight to the restroom, leaving Brenna to lounge about nearby. The place was empty but for a skinny cashier with horn-rim glasses and a big, grizzly-looking fellow whose T-shirt proclaimed him to be the best lover in all of Tennessee. He was helping himself to coffee from a stained pot, but gave the impression that he may well be past the point where caffeine would influence the hangover he'd have in the morning.

Nevertheless, he drank his brew, swore when he burnt his tongue, and headed for the cashier. He was just passing the men's room when the door was pushed open.

It hit his hands, sloshing hot coffee onto him. Yelping, he plucked his shirt from his chest.

"Geez! Sorry," Nate said. "You all right?"

"What the hell y' think yer doing?"

"Didn't know you were there. Can I get you something?" Nathan asked.

"Get me something?" Snorting, the big guy tossed his cup aside. Coffee splashed in every direction as he stepped up close to Nathan. "Yeah, you can get the hell out of my way, pretty boy, or you can get that cute little face of yours smashed in."

Nate straightened slightly, but Brenna could wait no longer. Sliding in between them, she spread her hands peaceably out to her sides.

"We'll pay for the coffee, mister," she said.

His eyes snapped open as he turned them down to her. She noticed when he grinned that his teeth were not very pretty. "This your little gal, pretty boy?"

"Move aside, O'Shay," Nathan said softly.

But Brenna remained where she was. "Listen." She raised her chin slightly. "We don't want any trouble here."

The big man's jaw dropped. "You protecting him?" he asked. She didn't answer, and he threw back his head and laughed. "Damn, this beats all," he guffawed, and reaching out, tried to swipe her aside.

Brenna had no choice but to give him a quick knuckle punch to the belly. He stumbled back, then, drunk and stupid, he came at them with a roar.

Panic sprang up in Brenna. But along with Master Leong's endless witticisms, he had given her repeated practical advice—when in serious physical peril, aim for the head and pray.

She was whirling before she could form a coherent thought. Her foot hit the side of grizzly man's cranium with an audible thud. He careened sideways like a drunken sailor, bounced once against the wall, and dropped to the floor like a crushed rag doll.

Absolute silence filled the shop.

"Oh, God." Paul Grand stood some feet away, his mouth open and his eyes wide. "Oh, God," he repeated.

By the time they left the shop, the fat guy was sitting up and Nathan had long since been hustled from the store, lest someone get the bright idea of suing.

The rest of the journey to Mena was filled with the boys' ribbing. They placed bets about pitting Brenna against various colorful characters ranging from Jackie Chan to Roger Rabbit.

She couldn't help but laugh at their attitudes, for though they teased her relentlessly, they obviously resented neither her ability nor her vocation.

Over an hour had passed before Brenna realized Nathan had barely said a word. Even when they disembarked at a small hotel and Brenna searched his room, he did little more than bid her good-night.

THE FOLLOWING DAY WENT SMOOTHLY. Brenna checked out the open-air concert area where The Cowboys would be performing and spoke with the local guards. Rain clouds threatened, so Brenna asked the road manager to check all the electrical wires once more, just to make sure they were safe.

The precaution paid off, for sure enough there was a small area that had cracked and was soon repaired.

When Nathan Fox rose to the stage, the crowd came to its feet and Brenna's work began in earnest.

They packed up early the next day and drove forever. The view was monotonous, the weather dreary, but it gave Brenna a chance to finish reading all Nathan's mail. The glimmer of a theory was beginning to form in her mind, but as of yet it hadn't bloomed. Daddy had been a big believer in intuition, and intuition needed time to blossom.

They reached Fort Worth by early evening, had a quick dinner and retired to the hotel.

THE FOLLOWING DAY FLEW BY. The Cowboys' performance went without a hitch. Brenna escorted Nathan to his room, which looked perfectly safe. She turned to exit it, but he stood between her and the door, his arms crossed against his chest.

"Ever dance?"

"What?" His words startled her. He had barely spoken to her for days on end, though she rarely left his side. She assured herself that it hadn't bothered her.

"Do you ever go dancing?"

"I, um…" Why did he always make her feel like some teenage hick? "I'm not much of a dancer."

"You should let the man lead sometimes."

"What?"

"It might make it simpler if you'd let your date lead."

She straightened, recognizing the anger in his eyes. "If you've got a problem with how I'm doing my job, Fox, spit it out, but I'd appreciate it if you'd leave my personal life alone."

"Personal life?" He snorted and took a step forward. "I'm willing to bet you don't have a personal life. When was the last time you went out?"

"Went out?" Already she felt backed against a wall, though she hadn't moved.

"Yeah. On a date."

She opened her mouth to reply, but he stopped her.

"You can't count strapping on a black belt and punching guys in the face."

"Oh." She lifted her chin. "Well, that narrows it down considerably then, Fox. 'Cause that's what I do for fun."

"I noticed."

"Listen." Anger was rising up in her. She'd been hired to do this job, and she was doing it damn well. "I didn't ask you to run into that oversized Tennessee Neanderthal."

"And I didn't ask you to kick him in the head."

"No, Sarge did. He hired a bodyguard. I'm a bodyguard."

He took another step toward her. "And what about a woman?"

She swallowed and raised her head to maintain eye contact. "What?"

"Are you a woman, too?"

"It doesn't matter, Fox. Not to you."

"'Fraid you're wrong there, sweetheart."

"If you need another notch in your bedpost, bubba, you're barking up the wrong tree," she warned. Someone had once told her that the white trash in her came out when she got mad.

"'Cause you're scared?" Fox asked.

Her jaw dropped, then she laughed. "I think you're forgetting who kicked fat guy's butt back there."

"Oh, you're not afraid of getting down and dirty," Fox said, stepping forward. "You're afraid of getting up close and personal."

"Huh?" She backed up a pace.

"You're afraid of intimacy."

She swallowed but tried to look nonchalant. "A little dime-store psychology, Fox?" she asked, mimicking his question from only days before.

"You're afraid to get close to me."

She snorted and took a step around him. "It's gonna be a long day tomorrow. Hook the chain behind me."

"O'Shay." Reaching out, he placed a palm against the door.

She stood trapped against the jamb, her heart leaping in her chest.

"You're scared," he murmured.

"The hell I am."

"Kiss me then."

"What?" She squashed her shoulder against the wall.

"Give me one kiss."

"I'm not afraid."

He grinned. "I'm giving you a chance to prove yourself." He shrugged. "It's more than you gave me with Fat Guy."

"What do y' mean by that?"

"You can set the rules."

"This is ridiculous."

"Want to set a time limit? A no-hands rule?"

"I want to go to bed."

His brows shot up. "Seems a little sudden. But it's okay by me."

Her face felt like it was heated by a blowtorch. "I'm leaving."

"You're never going to overcome that fear if you don't face it."

"I've been kissed before."

"Have you?"

In fact, she had once been engaged. For a while she had actually believed David could accept her dreams beyond the secretarial pool. But that illusion had shattered quickly enough. In the end, it had been quite ugly. The word "butch" was not one she was particularly fond of.

"Move your hand, Fox," she said.

"Or you're going to kick me in the head?"

"I'd rather not."

"I'm flattered. One kiss to show my appreciation."

"For?"

"For saving my life." He leaned slightly closer. His fingers brushed hers on the doorknob. And against all her better judgment, she could feel his presence spark through her like lightning down a rod.

"If I kiss you…" Just the thought made her brain start to sizzle. "*Once.* If I kiss you once, do you promise to quit this foolishness?"

He made a cross against his chest. "If you don't like it, I'll never ask again."

"Promise?"

"You bet. I'd die of shock anyway."

"Where do you get that ego?"

"I take it IV, directly into my bloodstream. What do you say?"

Her mind said this was the most adolescent thing she'd done since she'd engaged in spitting contests with her brothers. Her body, on the other hand, said if she didn't take advantage of this situation she was dumber than a mud fence in a rainstorm.

"All right, then. One kiss," she said.

He grinned that satyr's grin and leaned closer.

"But!" She scrunched back. "Then you won't bother me again?"

"You'll have to beg me," he said, leaning in.

"And just…" She was breathing too hard, and she'd barely eaten all day. It would be damned embarrassing if she passed out before he even touched her. It'd probably be a dead giveaway that she was a little bit nervous. "And just my lips."

"Where else did you have in mind?" he asked and lifted his hand toward her cheek.

"No!" She cleared her throat and licked her lips. "Hands by your sides."

He did as requested. "Ready?"

No! She nodded.

He smiled into her eyes, tilted his head, and kissed her.

Lightning flashed just behind her eyeballs, searing her nerve endings and turning her brain to cinders. Sensations tingled from her lips, scampering off in every direction, setting off a thousand alarm bells. Her knees went weak and her toes curled in her tennis shoes.

An instantaneous eternity passed. But finally Brenna realized he had drawn away and was watching her face. She opened her eyes and noted with some horror that she was plastered against the wall like spattered paint. Her knees were shaking and her head felt light, but she had her pride. Somewhere. She searched for it frantically for a moment, then, "Am I allowed to leave now?"

He watched her, his eyes slightly narrowed, and then he nodded once.

"Fine." She peeled her back from the wall, hoping all her body parts came with her, hoping the steam coming from her brain wasn't visible, hoping her knees remembered which way to bend. "Hook the chain behind me," she reminded him, and left.

A LUMBERJACK.

Nathan took another swig of his drink. He could be a lumberjack. That was a manly job. And he liked trees.

He finished his whiskey, straight up, and motioned for another.

Or a road mender. Standing out there deflecting traffic in blaze orange. A man's man.

A truck driver. The good thing about being a truck driver was that he could get really butt-ugly fat and no one would give a damn. In fact, it was probably a requirement for truck drivers.

A professional bull rider. He nodded at his suddenly empty glass. He'd done some bull riding and planned to do more. It was scary as hell. But nobody would think he was a wimp once his nose had been broken a half-dozen times. Even little Miss O'Sashay would think him a real man.

Geez! A bodyguard! A woman bodyguard. And now…now he couldn't even kiss. And it wasn't as if O'Shay was some movie star or something. She was a small-town kind of girl. Although she mulishly refused to talk about her upbringing, he guessed her roots weren't all that different from his. But he wasn't even man enough to tempt her.

Damn. When he was ranching, he may have worked his tail off, but at least when he had some time off, he could raise a spark or two with the hometown girls.

What the hell had happened to him? His dad had been right all along. The music business did turn men into pansies. Come morning he'd be plucking petals out of his ears.

Nathan took another swig, but the glass was dry. He scowled, licked the rim, and motioned for another.

The bartender was quick. He liked that in a bartender. Maybe he should be a bartender, he thought, and glanced toward the man's retreating back. But his attention was snagged by a woman perched on one of the high stools.

Legs. The woman had legs, he thought, then chuckled to himself, because most women had legs. He drank again and turned his eyes back to her. Her hair was red, and from the back she looked like…

It couldn't be! O'Shay couldn't have followed him, he thought wildly, then scoffed at himself. Geez! What was wrong with him? If he wanted to slip out alone for a private drink, he'd damn well do it. She wasn't his mother...or his wife...or his lover.

Damn.

The woman at the bar turned toward him. It wasn't O'Shay. Nate made a mental note to be happy about that and raised his glass to her. He was surprised when a goodly portion of the liquid sloshed across his fingers.

She had a nice body, shapely, a little full in the hips but, hey, he was going to be a truck driver.

Another sip.

She had a pretty face. But the really good thing about her was...she probably hadn't kicked anyone in the head all day.

The memory of his own bodyguard sent a hot wave of emotion through him. He slapped his glass to the table and stood up to leave, but as he did so, his gaze lifted to the woman at the bar once more.

She smiled at him. He grinned back, though her smile did nothing for him, no sparks of emotion, no sweaty hands, nothing.

But suddenly the man beside her stood up. He was big as a Brahma bull and not half so friendly looking. His lips were drawn back in a snarl and as he sauntered toward Nathan, fatty muscles rolled up his bare arms and over his neck.

Grinding to a halt not twelve inches from Nathan, he dropped his head between his shoulder blades like a hunting vulture and said, "You starin' at my woman, pretty boy?"

Nathan grinned. Testosterone, hot as hell and sharp as ice, flared through his system. "As a matter of fact, I am," he said in his very best Yankee accent. "She's not bad-looking...for a Texas gal."

7
___

"NATHAN!" BRENNA FLEW across the barroom and fell to her knees. "Nathan."

Her hands shook as she touched his face. His nose was bleeding, his cheek was cut, and his shirt was torn and bloody.

"Nathan, what happened?"

He grinned up at her. "Been fightin'."

"I'm going to call the police."

"No!" He caught her hand and pulled her back down beside him.

"I tried to break it up," said the bartender. Brenna turned to him. He was a big, apologetic-looking man. "I told 'em I was calling the cops. But that MacKenzie, it was like he was crazy."

"He had a friend," Nathan said. His grin had not diminished an iota.

Brenna felt tears prick her eyes. She'd heard of people getting so badly wounded that they became delirious. "I'm sorry," she whispered. "I should have found you earlier."

"*Big* friend," Nate said.

"They call him Viking," the bartender added. "He's worse than MacKenzie."

"Yeah." Nathan sighed. "I think he broke my nose."

"God, Nathan, not your nose." Brenna's fingers trembled against his cheek.

"They carried him out," Nate added. "Big fat lugger. I'm gonna get fat." He sighed as if content with the world.

"Where are the police?" Brenna asked, all but sobbing.

"This ain't such a good part of town, miss," the bartender said. "Sometimes they's a little slow."

"Call an ambulance."

"Don't want an ambulance," Nathan said. "The guy had a right hook like the kick of a mule. Damn near knocked me clear out of Texas."

"I'm going to get you to a hospital."

"How'd you find me?" he asked.

She noticed that when he looked at her, his eyes didn't quite focus and hoped it was because he was intoxicated and not because his brains had been pulverized into mashed bananas. Although, when she'd first realized he was gone, she'd threatened to do just that herself.

After the kiss, she'd spent the first half hour trying to figure out how to operate her knees. The second had been spent pacing. Finally, she'd tried to sleep, but there had been little hope of that.

In the end, her pride in tatters, and her hormones torqued into overdrive, she'd gone to his room.

When Brenna had rushed down to the front desk, the woman there had remembered Nathan, even though he hadn't used his real name. He'd said he needed a drink in a good old boys' bar. The rest had been easy enough. It hadn't taken a top-notch detective to find him in a town of ten thousand.

"Where's the nearest hospital?" she asked the bartender.

"Don't need a hospital," Nathan slurred.

"Listen, Fox—"

"You listen, O'Say." He chuckled at his own mistake. "O'Say," he said again. "Ohhh say can you see by the stars in my head." He laughed then, until he was crunched up on the floor, favoring his ribs. "Oh God. Whew, I feel good."

"Call an ambulance."

"You call an ambulance, you won't never see me again, sweetheart," Nathan said.

"And where would you go?"

"I'd ssslip right out of there." He nodded. "Become a truck driver." He said it like a small boy dreaming big dreams.

"You need your head examined."

"Yup. Take me to my room, O'Say. I think I'm tired."

"I think you're stupid."

"Yup. But I'm a man."

THE TAXI RIDE WAS SHORT and not too horrific. The trip across the hotel lobby and up to his room was worse. But finally they reached Nathan's door. Brenna slipped the key into the lock and helped him inside.

He crawled onto the bed, rested a moment, and finally flopped over on his back. Brenna stared down at him for a moment.

He stared back, one eye swollen half shut. "Bet you find me attractive now, huh?" he said.

She swallowed the lump in her throat. "I'm sorry," she murmured.

"'Bout this?" He motioned vaguely toward his face. "This is nothing. Once when I was riding bulls..." He paused to catch either his breath or his line of thought—she couldn't tell which. "I got throwed good. Knocked me senseless for a second. By the time I got to my feet...woosh." He made a sweeping motion with his hand. "Bull hooked me like I was a sunfish."

Brenna winced and eyed his chest. Several buttons had been wrenched from his shirt during the melee, and she was tempted nearly beyond control to brush her fingers across the exposed skin. "Is that where you got the scar?" she asked.

"Yeah." He grinned and rubbed his scar as if inordinately proud. "Nice one, huh? Got another rodeo in August. Wanna come and see me take a beating?"

Tears suddenly stung her eyes. "I'll get a washcloth," she said, and hurried away.

A minute later, with her emotions under better control, she returned with an ice bucket half filled with cold water and settled her hip on the edge of the mattress. He watched her face as she gently dabbed the blood from his nose. The room was silent.

"So why aren't you married, Ms. O'Say?" he asked.

She cleared her throat and hoped she wouldn't cry. "Why aren't you?"

He shook his head, then scowled as if any quick movement wasn't such a good idea. "Life on the road," he said. "Tough. Rover's been divorced twice. Did you know that? Never sees his kids. And Fry. Once. What kind of woman'd want to buy into this kinda life?"

She remained quiet for a moment, but it seemed to be an honest question, so she answered finally. "Quite a few, I'd think."

He snorted. "Yeah. But what *kind?* They're—" he sighed "—not like Mom. Shauna…I thought she was. 'Course, I stole her from Sarge in the first place, so I suppose he's got a right to be a pain in the ass. But they're back together, you know."

His eye looked horrible. God, she'd made a mess of things. "No." She sniffed. "I didn't know."

He nodded. "'Course he doesn't see her much, seein's how he's married to his clipboard. Him and Shauna were singing together before I ever hooked up with them. They were set on making it big. But—"

"What?"

He grinned. "Sarge says *he* grew up. Now he baby-sits me. Surprised me he could give up the dream."

"Of being a star?"

"Yeah. Damn dream's got a bite like a damned sheepdog. Most guys can't give it up without getting bitter."

"How about Shauna?" She knew she shouldn't ask. There was probably nothing lower than prodding a man for information when he was drunk.

"She's a nurse in Nebraska. She used to be good though. When I first saw her on stage…" He sighed. "She was a country gal. Wheat farmers. Can ride horse and everything."

She let the words lie there, but she couldn't hold back the question for long. "You're still in love with her?" The question didn't sound quite so innocuous as she'd intended.

But Nathan merely turned his gaze to the ceiling. "If I

was sober I'd say naw. But I'm sauced. Maybe you couldn't tell.''

"I thought maybe."

"Yeah, I'm drunk as a skunk. I mean, I'm sloppy drunk. So I don't know. Could be I still got feelings for her, or maybe I'm still in love with the idea."

"What idea?"

"Of having a woman. A woman who cares, you know, 'bout *me*. Not about The Fox. 'Bout me.''

Somehow his wrist had flopped over her thigh, and her hip was pressed quite firmly against his waist. His dark hair was damp and brushed away from his bruised forehead, and his discolored face looked painfully vulnerable.

"You think that's too much to ask, O'Shay? Love, marriage, maybe a couple of kids that call me dad. Or *daddy* like you say down here. Ty and Hannah, they got them a little daughter—Amanda," he said dreamily. "If I had me a daughter I'd spoil her rotten."

He made it sound achingly sweet. Her heart did a painful little twist in her chest. But it wasn't her dream, not her dream at all. *This* was her dream—to be in law enforcement, to prove herself. She swallowed and didn't even try to talk.

He lifted his hand to her cheek and brushed his nail pads, soft as thistledown, against her cheek. She closed her eyes to the shiver of feelings.

"I can imagine you as a little girl," he whispered. "All giggles and hugs. Little…" He thought for a moment, his expression somber, his eyes intense. "Brenda? Bonnie? Bridget?" he guessed.

She didn't help him out, but he didn't seem to care.

"Your daddy must of been so proud he could bust.''

She closed her eyes, trying to hold back the emotions, but it was no use. He drew out some horribly weak part deep inside her. There was no hope for it. Leaning forward, she touched her lips to his.

He slipped a hand behind her neck, urging her gently closer. The caress deepened. Brenna's heart slammed against the hard plane of his chest. She trembled in his arms. His fingers slipped over her shoulder, down her arm…and fell to the bed.

She started, glanced at his hand, limp against the coverlet, then hurried her gaze to his face.

Damn it all. He was asleep.

"FOX." BRENNA KNOCKED LIGHTLY on his door. It was only seven in the morning. But she'd been up for hours. Now, showered, dressed, and composed, she swore she could face him like a professional. She knocked again. "Fox?"

"If you don't have a medical diploma, go away."

"Fox," she called again, but he didn't answer, so she pushed her key into his lock and let herself in.

He was sitting on the edge of the bed and glanced up when she stepped into his sleeping quarters. He looked like hell.

"How do I look?"

"Not bad," she lied.

He laughed, but it sounded rather like a croak. "You ought to take lying lessons, O'Shay. I look like hell."

"I wouldn't say hell…exactly."

He dropped his face gently back into his hands and chuckled.

She grinned and stepped forward. "I brought you something."

"Is it a forty-five?"

"I don't think suicide's the answer."

"You're right, I might as well just wait and die a natural death. I don't think it'll be much longer."

"Here." She sat down beside him and nudged his elbow with the ceramic cup she held in her hand.

He peeked at it through his swollen eye. "What is it?"

"My secret weapon for hangovers."

"You an expert?"

"Kind of. My brothers liked for me to play nurse."

"You got brothers?"

"Five of them. All big-drinking Irishmen and not a casualty yet."

"Yeah?" He straightened slightly, trying to see into the

cup. But she kept the top carefully covered with her hand. "What's in it?"

"I told you it's a secret. You have to drink it all right down."

"Then I'll be cured?"

"Well, pretty soon."

"Promise?"

He looked pathetic. Almost pathetic enough to make her warn him that the cure was nearly as bad as the malady. "Promise," she said.

"Okay." He reached for the cup.

"Plug your nose."

"Huh?"

"Plug your nose. Swallow it all."

"Got it," he said, took the cup, downed the contents, then sat there with his eyes as big as dinosaur eggs as he gasped for breath.

Brenna pried the cup from his fingers, then quickly stood and cleared a path to the bathroom.

It took only a couple of seconds before he launched from the bed and sprang for the toilet.

Brenna turned her back and made faces at the wall as disgusting sounds echoed through the room. Finally, there was a lull, then the sound of running water and tooth-brushing.

Nearly five minutes passed before Nathan emerged. He dragged himself to the bed, curled up on the mattress, and stared blankly at the wall. "It was you, wasn't it?"

Brenna stepped carefully closer. She'd learned early on that some people appreciated her cure more than others. "Me what?"

"You sent the letters, didn't you? You're the one trying to kill me."

She laughed a little. "It's not that bad. Really. You'll feel better in a minute."

"I'll be dead in a minute," he croaked.

Nervously, she sat back down on the mattress. "I wanted to apologize."

"So I really am going to die?"

She smiled, knowing she shouldn't sit so close. Knowing she was playing with fire and was fresh out of asbestos. "I, um...I think I was overzealous."

The room was silent.

"At the gas station," she added. "I shouldn't have decked that guy." She glanced at his muscular torso where his shirt flopped open, baring far too much skin for her to think properly. "I know you could have handled him. It's just that..." She let out a breath. "Sometimes people don't take me seriously. Y' know...my being a bodyguard. It could be I've been trying too hard."

Nathan remained as he was for a moment, then reached up to gently brush his knuckles along her cheek. "Could be I've been acting like an ass," he said, his voice a soft caress.

Desire sparked through her. She looked away, trying to calm her hormones, but that was about as effective as a garden hose on an inferno. "I was thinking we could start over."

"Good idea," he murmured.

One kiss. Just one kiss, her mind whispered. She shushed the nasty little voice. "On a strictly professional basis."

He brushed the ridge of her lower lip with his thumb. A shiver ran through her, fine as gossamer.

"Professional," he whispered.

"I'm, um..." She tried to keep breathing as his fingers skimmed her jaw then ran up the outer shell of her ear. "I'm your bodyguard."

"Right."

His hand slipped beneath her hair. Brenna closed her eyes to the delicious feelings.

"We won't let it be anything else," she whispered.

"Of course not." He gently urged her closer.

She was breathing hard through her parted lips. "No matter how badly I want to."

"I want to, too," he murmured, and she was lost. His lips touched hers.

"Fox." Knuckles rapped on the door a moment before it was swung open.

Brenna jumped like a cat from a skillet. The cup flew out

of her hand, bounced off the wall, and landed spinning on the carpet.

"Whoa!" Fry said, his eyebrows out of sight.

"This isn't...I didn't... This isn't what it seems," Brenna stuttered.

"Really?" If Fry's grin got any bigger, his head would split wide open.

"I just... Nathan needed... He wasn't..." Brenna took a deep breath and momentarily wished she were dead. "I brought him some medicine."

"Really? You sick, Nate?"

Nathan stared point blank at the fiddler. "Why are you here, Fry?"

Surprisingly, his grin could get bigger. "Sarge says it's time to hit the road."

"Oh, yeah. I'll just...I'll get my things," Brenna said, and torpedoed from the room.

THE NEXT THREE DAYS PASSED in a blur of necessary activities. They were on the road for long hours, allowing Brenna to draw away from Fox's side while still knowing he was safe.

Nathan played with lyrics, Brian spent time on the phone with his wife, and Nuf, true to his usual demeanor, fell off the top of the couch twice and once got his claw caught in the ring of a soda can. He clanked around for a good five minutes before anyone saved him from further humiliation.

As for Brenna, she skimmed letters, studied maps, contemplated agendas, contacted a dozen security agencies, and absolutely refused to relive those few moments when Nathan's lips had touched her own.

She was his bodyguard. His bodyguard! Nothing else. He was her employer, she reminded herself repeatedly. Each time she was forced to address him, she maintained as much physical and emotional distance as possible between them, calling him Mr. Fox, and refusing, absolutely refusing, to touch him unless there was no alternative.

Somewhere between Fort Worth and Albuquerque they

had a tire blowout. The delay threw them off schedule. By the time they reached Phoenix, Nathan had to rush to his first interview, followed by a stint with a radio station. Brenna went with him. While he was on the air, she contacted Atlas to check on the condition of the buses and insist that they be completely checked over by a reliable mechanic.

The remainder of the afternoon was just as hectic—an autographing session at a local mall, a picture with the mayor.

After Nathan's final obligation, it was nearly dark. Brenna positioned herself as far from him as possible and tried to pretend he was short and balding and fat. But her imagination had never been that good.

Slumped against the corner of the limousine, Brenna watched Nathan pull an envelope from his pocket and thumb through a pile of photographs in the waning light.

"Which one do you like?" he asked, handing her the pictures.

Brenna took the stack from his hand. Each photograph boasted a horse, all pintos, though some were professional shots and some obviously amateur.

"A new purchase?" she asked, glancing up.

He shook his head. "Jack Simmons' horses. For a video shoot."

"I thought you had a ranch, complete with horses and everything."

"Yeah, well..." He glanced out the window. "I don't have paint horses, and paint horses are the up-and-coming thing. Fastest growing breed in America. Sarge said if they put me on a paint horse folks'll notice."

Brenna laughed. But when Nathan turned to her, his face was sober, though somewhat quizzical.

"I'm sorry." She felt foolish, fatigued and underfed. She was going to have to remember to eat more. Because when her blood sugar dropped, she had a propensity for making a fool of herself. "I thought you were joking."

"Joking?"

Sweet Mary, he was beautiful, his face chiseled and shadowed. Suddenly there seemed little reason to pretend otherwise. "They're not going to notice the color of your horse," she said.

His expression softened a little. "Is that a compliment, O'Shay?"

"No!" A little too sharp. She was more tired than she'd realized. "I'm just saying, I don't see what difference the color of the horse would make."

He grinned a little. "So you think I could ride my own mare?"

There wasn't a woman in America who'd give a rip if he put on a sackcloth and rode a damn camel. As long as they could stare at him they'd be thrilled, Brenna thought, but found enough control to keep her foolish ideas to herself.

"It's not my area," she said. "I'm sure Sarge knows what he's doing."

Nathan shrugged. "He's never cared much about horses."

She said nothing and turned carefully back toward the window. Looking at him when her inhibitions were down was not such a good idea. And the thought of him on horseback did bad things to her libido. When she was ten she'd begun taping pictures of horses up on her wall. When she was twelve she switched to pictures of cowboys. But her favorites had always been cowboys *on* horses.

"How 'bout you?"

"What?" She nearly jumped, then sternly reminded herself that he could not read her mind. He didn't know that they shared a common interest. And it would stay that way, allowing her to maintain her distance.

"Do you know horses?"

"No."

He stared at her. He *couldn't* read her mind. Could he?

"Well." She cleared her throat. "You know—girls and horses. They're supposed to be inseparable."

"Yeah." He grinned. "Why do you think I rodeo?"

She tried to turn away, but he was…well…breathing. And that seemed to be all that was necessary to snare her attention. "To impress the cowgirls?" she guessed.

"You got it. Skippa Lula, she's—"

"You have a Skipper horse?"

He stared at her. "You know more about horses than you're telling, O'Shay."

Damn. There was something wrong with her. "I just..." She shrugged, feeling stupid. "A friend of mine's momma raised quarter horses."

"Yeah?"

"Yeah. I helped out sometimes. At shows and stuff. Then they'd let me ride Pineapple."

"Palomino, I bet," he guessed.

She smiled, both at his deduction and at the memories. "He was older than dirt, but I loved him. When my brothers wouldn't—" She stopped herself abruptly.

The silence was heavy as a rock.

"I think you can tell me a little about yourself without the risk of being attacked, O'Shay. Maybe even your name."

She didn't offer.

"This is a strictly professional relationship, remember?" he said.

"The story just isn't very interesting."

"Really? Why don't you tell it to me then? Maybe it'll put me to sleep. When your brothers wouldn't what?"

"Oh, look at the fountain," she said, turning to stare at the lighted cascade of water. But she couldn't avoid his gaze forever.

"When they wouldn't what?" he repeated.

She shrugged, hoping she looked irritable. "I was the only girl. They got tired of playing with me."

"Don't think that'd be possible," he murmured.

She drew herself straighter. "Mr. Fox—"

He lifted his hands as if in surrender. "Just trying to pass the time, O'Shay. I think of you in professional terms only." He said to the driver, "You can pull up to that first bus."

The chauffeur did so, sweeping around a turn and coming to a halt a few feet from the tour bus.

Brenna stepped out of the car first. Nathan spoke a few words to the driver, then followed her out.

In a moment, the limo pulled away.

Brenna's jaw dropped. "Aren't we going to the hotel?"

"I don't feel like eating restaurant food. Thought maybe I'd do some cooking. Then if you want, we could sleep here."

"I can't stay alone with—" she began frantically, then stopped herself. "I mean, I think it would be safer to—"

He grinned as he ushered her toward the bus. "I trust you."

"What?"

"To protect me," he said, opening the door.

"Oh." She'd thought he meant he trusted her not to take advantage of him, but maybe even *he* wasn't *that* foolish. She stepped into the bus, and he followed.

"I am safe with you, aren't I?" he asked.

"Of course, you—" she began to say, but just then she noticed the laughter in his tone. She turned toward him, peeved and fatigued.

It was then that the shadow lurched over her.

8

THE SHADOW LOOMED OVER BRENNA, a huge crooked figure, an extended arm. A gun! Brenna froze, terror choking her. She'd been careless, distracted. And now it was too late.

"Time's up, Fox."

His words mimicked Brenna's thoughts, mocking her. And it was those words that tore her from her paralysis. Spinning desperately about, she slammed her heel into the attacker's hand. His gun flew sideways. She swiveled in, grabbed his arm, and yanked him over the top of her bent body.

He grunted. Nuf yowled, and Nate shouted. But Brenna delayed not a moment. Dodging in, she pounced atop the intruder, her hands drawn back and ready to strike lest he make the slightest move.

"O'Shay!" Nathan yelled. "Are you all..." He switched the light on, and his words trailed off.

"Call the police," she gasped, her gaze not leaving the attacker for a moment.

"What—" the villain began.

"Shut up!" She repeated to Nathan, "Call the police!"

"But..."

"Not now. He may have another weapon."

"Another?" Nathan cleared his throat and stepped closer. "Another weapon?"

"Stay back! Leave the gun where it's at."

"Gun?"

She scowled, but didn't take her gaze from the attacker. "If you're feeling woozy, sit down, Fox, but for God's sake, call the police."

"All right. But I need to ask one question. Why are you sitting on my brother?"

She opened her mouth to snap out an answer. It was then that she realized her mistake, that she saw the family resemblance.

The man she was sitting on was, perhaps, a few years older than Nathan, and his hair was a couple of shades darker, but they shared the same chiseled features, the same hard-bodied physique. Beneath her buttocks, abdominal muscles bunched like an angry bull's.

"Your..." She couldn't force out the word for a moment, and chanced a glance at Nathan. He stood with his arms crossed. "Your brother?"

"Tyrel."

She winced. "You're sure?"

"Pretty sure." He nodded almost apologetically. "Tyrel, meet B. T. O'Shay. O'Shay, Ty."

"But..." She flickered her attention back to the face of the fellow beneath her. Oh no. Not another person to scurry out of her way every time she walked by. "But you had a gun," she murmured.

"Gun?" His voice still sounded a little guttural, but in all fairness, that may have been because she was sitting on his stomach.

She glanced to her left. "The gun I knocked out of your..." Oh no. A baseball cap lay at a cocked angle against the bathroom door. If she really stretched her imagination, she could see how the crooked shadow of the brim could have looked like the snubbed nose of a Beretta.

"You said, 'Time's up, Fox,'" she murmured weakly.

Tyrel stared at her for a moment. "I said, ''Bout time you got back, Fox.'"

"Oh." She cleared her throat and wondered if there were any way to look casual while sitting on a man's abdomen. "How'd you get in here?"

"Nate gave me a key a coupla years back."

"A key?" she gasped, flipping her appalled gaze to Nathan.

He shrugged. "He's my brother."

"And you didn't tell me?"

"Slipped my mind."

"My God, Fox, I could have…" She gestured wildly.

"Killed me?" Tyrel guessed.

She searched for words for a moment, then gave up. "Made a fool of myself," she muttered weakly.

Nathan chuckled.

Tyrel grinned.

"What are you doing down here, Ty?" Nathan asked, squatting down as if this were an everyday type of conversation.

"She's sitting on me."

"I mean in Texas."

"Oh. Hannah's competing all over with Maverick this year. They jump tomorrow in Dallas."

"Yeah? Where's Mandy?"

"She's with her mom. God knows you can't get her away from the horses," Ty said and winced.

"Maybe you'd better get off him," Nathan said. "He's not as young as he used to be."

"Oh!" Brenna stumbled to her feet. "I just…" Bending quickly, she jerked his cap from the floor and handed it to him. "I thought…"

Tyrel rose more slowly, glanced at Brenna's warm face, then turned his gaze to his brother.

There was a moment of silence, then a shrug from Nate. "She's my bodyguard."

More silence. "Huh?"

A self-effacing grin. That one that made Brenna forget that Nathan Fox was the kind of chauvinistic pain in the ass she detested.

"Yep. She's here to guard my body."

"From what?"

Nathan shrugged as he turned toward the fridge. "Sarge is fretting. What the hell were you doing sitting here in the dark?"

"I fell asleep. About what?"

"About what, what?" Nathan asked.

"What is Sarge fretting about?"

"You name it. We got a couple of Buds. Want one?"

"Nate, what's going on?"

Nathan turned toward Brenna, still bent double. "You want anything?" he asked, his derriére inches from her.

"No." She wrenched her gaze from his tighter-than-sin behind and tried not to squirm. "Thank you."

"What the hell's going on?" Tyrel demanded.

"Geez, Ty," Nate said, toeing the fridge closed and sauntering over to the long couch that lined one wall. "You get tossed on your can by a woman and you don't turn a hair. But I tell you Sarge is fretting and you go haywire."

"Since meeting Hannah, being tossed on my can is the least of my problems. What's Sarge worried about?"

Nathan shrugged noncommittally. "It's nothing."

"Then why's he worried? He ain't as dumb as he looks, you know."

Nathan laughed as he plopped onto the couch and screwed the top off his beer. "That'd almost have to be true."

"What's up?" Ty asked, all seriousness now.

"Nothing." Nathan took a swig.

Ty turned his gaze to Brenna.

She felt like backing away with her hands in the air. "I'm in Mr. Fox's employ," she said.

Tyrel scowled at her, and looked for all the world like an exact replica of his brother. "You just kicked me in the arm and threw me on my butt," he said. "Seems to me you owe me something."

Brenna would have liked to argue with that, but there was a certain amount of guilt that followed pouncing on an innocent man's stomach, so she cleared her throat and glanced at Nathan.

He scowled at her, but she ignored it. "There have been some inexplicable accidents."

"That's right. *Accidents!*" Nate said. "And nothing more."

"What accidents?"

"They're nothing," Nathan repeated. "A blown tire. An electrical short. On the farm we'd call that a good day."

"What about the time you were nearly run down while jogging?" Brenna asked.

"Who told you about that?"

"*Sarge* seems to think I should be aware of a few things." Nate shrugged. "We were in L.A.!"

Brenna paused, watching him. He was trying to look relaxed, but she could see the tension in his body. "How do you explain the letters?" she asked.

He tensed a bit more.

"What letters?" Tyrel's voice was low.

"They're nothing."

"He's been getting threatening letters for more than a year."

"From who?"

"That's what I'm trying to figure out."

"So I get a couple of letters that talk about something other than my good looks," Nathan said. He took another swig and grinned. "You can't blame men for being jealous when their women whisper my name in their sleep."

"Is that what you think?" Tyrel asked. "Someone's jealous enough to threaten you?"

"They're not threatening me," Nate said. "They're just a half-dozen letters that—"

"Ten," Brenna corrected.

"What?"

"There are ten letters. I found a few others. They were more subtle, but I think they're all from the same person."

"Hell, Nate! Why didn't you tell me?"

"Geez!" Nathan rose jerkily from the couch. "Tell you what? That some guy told me to be careful when I go running? That ain't all that significant, brother."

"Well, if somebody tries to run you down the next week it is."

"It wasn't the next week. And the letter was postmarked from Ohio. You think he followed me to L.A. to run me over?"

The bus went silent.

"Maybe you should come home and lie low for a while. Pansy could fuss over you. Give the kitchen floor a break. She's scrubbed it clean through to the basement."

For a moment Nathan looked as if he would retort, but finally he let out a breath and grinned. "How *is* Pansy?"

"Old, ornery, bossy."

"'Bout the same then," Nathan said.

The tension dissipated a little.

"The folk'd love to see you, Nate."

"I'll be there by August," Nathan said. "In plenty of time for the rodeo, so you'd better practice so you don't slow down my roping time."

"But if some guy—"

"No!" Brenna interrupted breathlessly.

Both men turned to her, and she started. She hadn't meant to say it out loud.

"What?" Nathan asked.

She let out a deep breath and stared at him. "I've been wrong all along."

"What are you talking about?" Nathan asked.

Suddenly energized and certain, Brenna rushed to the back of the bus and dragged a small bag of letters from the overhead cabinet.

In a moment, she had them all flipped open on the tabletop. "Look at this," she said, giddy with excitement. "Each one says something about your good looks." She skimmed them again, page after page. "Listen. 'You should cut your hair.' 'How do you keep in such great shape?' 'Wear dark colors.'"

"Don't know why, but Nate's always drawn the women," Tyrel said uncertainly.

She glanced up. "Those are signed with men's names."

"All right, that's weird," Ty said.

"They're from a woman," Brenna murmured.

Nathan scoffed, then shook his head as he stepped forward. "That's crazy."

"It's not. Who else would consistently talk about your looks?"

"You're imagining."

"They're really quick references," Brenna said, almost faint with excitement. "I didn't notice them at first either. But something's been worrying at me. I knew there was some kind of bond." She skimmed them quickly again. "What kind of man would say those things?"

"A really weird one," Ty said. "You been hanging around weird guys, Nate?"

"Since childhood. But you're my brother."

Ty ignored him, turning to Brenna. "What are you going to do now?"

She shook her head. "I don't know. Nothing immediately."

"You've got time for supper then," Tyrel said. "I could take you both out. We could mull it over."

"We just got in from out," Nathan said, abruptly turning his back on the letters. "Too bad Hannah's not here. She could cook us up something." He laughed, but the sound was a little stiff.

Brenna quickly scooped the mail back into the bag. She would love to pore over them, examine them yet again, but Nathan looked tired suddenly, and though he wouldn't admit it, she thought the letters bothered him. Time with his brother would do him more good than analyzing threatening mail.

"I'd rather starve to death in peace than eat Hannah's cooking," Tyrel said. "*Your* culinary talents improved any?"

"My cooking was good enough those first years at The Lone Oak."

"That was before Hannah hired Pansy. My taste buds have blossomed."

"Yeah, well, you're a redneck at heart," Nate said, and opened a door to scan his cupboards. "You'll adjust."

In the end they decided to make chili. Brenna secured the door, made sure all the shades were drawn, and saved Nuf from a half-opened kitchen drawer in which he'd gotten his fat head stuck searching for food. She pulled out a notebook and sat toward the back of the bus, giving the brothers as much privacy as possible. But despite her best intentions, it was impossible to ignore them.

True, she had grown up with five brothers, and thus she should be used to their rough comradery, but nevertheless, these two intrigued her. Unlike her brothers, who had refused to learn to do so much as stir soup, they leaned over the stove with relish, arguing about everything from spices to curing hay. The domesticity should have made them seem effeminate, she thought. But somehow, it did the opposite.

Seeing their rangy bodies stretch to look in the cupboard or flex to stash a bowl away, only made them seem more masculine. Nathan's big hand on the wooden ladle entranced her somehow.

Unfortunately, he glanced up just as she was staring at him. The sly corner of a grin touched his lips.

"Figured out who the author is yet, Sherlock?" he asked.

Maybe she should have been offended by his question. But she couldn't quite manage it. "Uh-huh."

"Yeah?" He quit his stirring.

"Sure." She knew she should stay put, keep her distance, but he looked so touchable and charming in his stocking feet and half grin. Rising, she ventured into the small kitchen. "But I can't tell you now or I'll be out of a job."

He chuckled.

"Ask *her*," Ty said.

"Ask me what?"

"Doesn't that need more chili powder?" Tyrel asked.

"If you have a fire hose handy," Nathan said. "Here." He scooped a bit of chili onto the wooden ladle and lifted it toward her.

Brenna backed away. Professionalism! she reminded herself firmly. She mustn't get too close to this guy, especially when he was like this, homey and real and so damned attractive it made her eyes water.

Nate looked questioningly at her.

"Cooking's not my field," she said, though actually she was a decent chef and rather enjoyed it.

"Ah, yes, the consummate bodyguard," Nathan said. "But you do eat." He pushed the spoon a little closer. "I saw you—just the day before yesterday you had a raisin."

She couldn't help but laugh.

"Taste it," he urged.

She finally did, chewing thoroughly before swallowing and scowling in thought.

"Well?" the brothers asked in unison.

"It needs more chili powder."

Her statement was the start of a whole new argument, but this time Brenna was drawn into it. It seemed that not a topic was left untouched, from cutting horses to the ozone layer.

Fifteen minutes later, when they sat down to eat, Nathan broached a new subject. "Sarge thinks I should rent one of Simmons' paints for the new video."

"Jack Simmons?"

"Yeah."

"You'd go way down to Oklahoma to ride a horse?"

"A *paint* horse. You know Sarge. Working every angle. Gotta go with the fads."

"Pay me half as much as you'd have to pay Simmons and you can ride one of mine," Ty said.

Nate snorted as he consumed the chili. "I could ride Lula for free."

"You don't want a palomino. You want a nice bay. Hazard's got—"

"Oh geez!" Nate said. "Spare me the litany of your stud's fine qualities."

Tyrel laughed. "What do you think, Brenna? Don't you think Nate should ride a brown horse? He's already so..." He gestured vaguely toward him with an open hand. "Don't you think he'd look kind of girly on a yellow horse?"

Brenna couldn't help but laugh at the noise Nathan made as he choked on his dinner.

"I've always had a fondness for palominos," she said.

"You know horses. She knows horses," Tyrel said in surprise.

"A small-town girl," Nate said.

"Yeah? A small-town bodyguard. I haven't had a need for a lot of bodyguards, but I'm guessing you're not the average sort," Ty observed.

"Better legs," Nate said and grinned.

Brenna stiffened slightly, wishing with all her might that she could work up a little righteous indignation. "I assure you I'm well trained and proficient," she said. "I'll take good care of your brother."

Ty grinned as he rubbed his arm where she'd kicked him. "I wasn't doubting."

She looked down and played with her crackers. "Oh. Well…" She rose to her feet and headed for the door. "I'm going to meander around the parking lot for a little while."

"O'Shay?"

"Yeah?" She turned back to Nathan.

"Don't attack anybody unless I'm there to watch, huh?"

She snorted as she left the bus, and both men grinned.

"Well," Ty said and rose to his feet. "I'd better get back. Much as I'm sure you'd like me to uh…" he leaned back to move a shade and glance out the window "…*chaperone*, I can't stay the night." His gaze skimmed back to Nate who rose too.

"I *will* miss you. The dishes aren't washed, and I'm scared to ask O'Shay to help."

Ty chuckled as he moved toward the door. He pulled on his boots then straightened. "You'll be careful, won't you?"

"What do you think, that I hired O'Shay for her great legs?"

"I know you better than that," Ty said. "Your tastes run higher up."

Nathan glanced toward the door. "If I reach in *that* direction, I'm liable to have my hand chewed off."

"It could be what you've needed all along, brother—a woman with teeth."

Nathan snorted. "What I need is a woman who can't beat me in arm wrestling."

Tyrel chuckled. "Maybe she'll let you win."

Nate thought of a snappy rejoinder, but didn't say it. Instead, he leaned his shoulder against the wall and stared at his older brother.

Silence filled the bus.

"That bad, huh?" Ty asked.

"What?" Nathan pulled away from the wall. "No. It's just…" He exhaled sharply and ran splayed fingers through his hair. "Damn, it's confusing. She looks like a lamb and kicks like a mule."

"Some folks swear by mules."

Nate sighed. "She don't want none of it, Ty."

"What *does* she want?"

Nathan shrugged. He didn't mean to act like a snot-nosed kid, but Tyrel seemed to bring out that side of him. There was nothing like a big brother to wipe your nose for you. "Maybe she wants to be a man." He felt grumpy and frustrated and knew he was being unfair.

"Yeah?" Ty said. "Well, if that's what she's after, she's losing the battle. And she don't look like no loser to me."

"What are you saying?"

"I'm saying, she's the best thing I've seen you with since you left your palomino at home, son."

Nathan shook his head. "She's all wrong for me."

"Too pretty?"

Nate snorted. "She's independent and stubborn and, hell, she drives me crazy. I need someone like…Mom. Someone who'll take care of me when—"

Tyrel laughed out loud. "Are you talking about *our* mom? The woman who took out the buggy whip when Dad came home drunk?"

"What?"

"Maybe you were too young to remember, little brother. But there's a reason Dad walks the straight and narrow."

Nathan remained quiet for a moment. "Are you saying I should go after O'Shay?"

"I'm saying—" Ty scooped his cap onto his head "—Dad's the one who swears by mules."

9

BRENNA CROUCHED UNDER Nathan's nightstand, fiddling with some wires and worrying about a thousand things. Who was sending the letters? Would her brothers leave her alone to do her job? Who had called Bartman Security to ask about her?

She pushed the last worry out of her mind. Because if anyone associated with Fox Inc. suspected she wasn't a certified bodyguard, she'd certainly have heard about it by now.

Which allowed her to worry about other things. She glanced toward the bed. But she refused to think how he would look lying there. She wouldn't think of how his fingers would feel against her skin, or how his voice would tickle her ear.

They hadn't slept on the bus three nights ago as Nathan had suggested, but had returned to the relative safety of the hotel. Still, she had known he slept in the very next room to hers, only a few feet away. The thought had made her queasy *last* night, but tonight was worse yet. She'd been unable to do anything more constructive than pace. Which was infinitely better than begging him to do what she was dying to beg him to do.

"What are you doing?"

Brenna jerked up at the sound of Nathan's voice, hitting her head on the ledge of the narrow nightstand. She rubbed the burgeoning bump, slipped onto his bed, and refused to blush, for she was certain she had nothing to feel guilty about.

"What are *you* doing?" she asked.

"I'm standing in my bus, wondering what the hell you're doing with your head stuck under my drawers."

"I've been hired to protect you, remember?" she said, standing up and trying not to fidget. She had snuck out here long after she was certain he would be asleep. Sure she would be undisturbed, she hadn't bothered with her professional image. Instead, she'd merely slipped into a pair of comfortable shorts and an oversized T-shirt. "Sarge gave me free rein."

"Free rein!" he scoffed as he leaned against the doorjamb. His bare arms looked tan and muscular where he'd torn the sleeves from his faded plaid shirt. "What are you, a trail horse? Guess that'd make me a wrangler—ready to cull the herd and gentle the keepers. You a keeper or a cull, O'Shay?"

The thing about Fox was, he shifted gears too fast, Brenna thought nervously. His emotions were as changeable as her underwear. She rushed to keep up.

"I'm not a horse," she said, feeling skittish.

"You must be a woman then, O'Shay. And I tell you what, if there's a beautiful woman spending time in my bed, I'd sure as hell like to be there when it happens."

She was *not* going to blush. "I wasn't spending time in your bed." She said the words very primly, and wished with all her soul that for once she could sound gruff. "I was installing a listening device."

"You're bugging my bedroom?" he asked, straightening from the wall.

She cleared her throat. "I've been hired to—"

"You're bugging my bedroom?" he repeated, louder now.

"I just want to make certain that if anyone breaks in we can—"

"Listen, sweetheart, if you want to know what goes on in my bedroom, you can just ask."

She raised her chin a notch. "You, Mr. Fox, have an ego of outstanding proportions."

"You should see my other attributes."

Snatching her bag of goodies from the bed where Nuf

sprawled, Brenna prepared to storm by Nathan, but he spoke again.

"Why the bedroom, O'Shay?" he asked. "Why such interest in here? The horrible villains could be anywhere. Under the sink. Over the cabinets. In the refrigerator!"

"Don't worry yourself about it," she said, pressing past him.

He turned with her, then snatched her arm at the last moment. "You bugged my refrigerator?"

"I've been hired to—"

"Dammit, O'Shay, you've been hired to keep Sarge from driving me crazy and look cute doing it. Nothing more."

"I've been hired to protect you," she ground out and jerked her arm from his grasp. "No matter how it batters your fragile, overblown ego."

"Overblown! Hell, woman, I'll be lucky to retain the tiniest germ of an ego by the time you're through. It's not bad enough that I need a woman to protect me, now you want me to believe it's a *woman* who's trying to kill me!"

"I don't write the letters, Fox. I just read them."

"Read them! You *pore* over them. You *immerse* yourself in them. You go to *bed* with them!"

She stiffened at the innuendo. "Is there a point you're trying to make, Fox?"

"How long ago did your job replace men in your life?"

"You've no right to pry into my private life."

"Private life," he scoffed and settled a shoulder against the doorjamb again. "O'Shay, I don't even know your first *name*, much less your private life." He paused, and though it seemed impossible, she thought she saw a flicker of laughter in his eyes. "Give me a little something."

"What?" She all but hissed the question.

He grinned. "A little morsel to chew on. Your name? Address? Shoe size?"

She pursed her lips and tried to remain strong, but his grin did evil things to her equilibrium. "I'm a bodyguard," she said stiffly. "That's all you need to know."

"Okay. Let's start there. Why do you do it?"

She would have backed off a pace, but there was no room. "What?"

"Why are you a bodyguard?"

"It's what I'm good at."

His gaze seemed warm and steady on her face. With his hat gone and his plaid shirt open several buttons, he looked casual and earthy and so ruggedly attractive it made her eyeballs sweat.

"I bet you're good at a lot of things," he said quietly.

"You might be surprised."

"With your looks and your tenacity you could be anything you want." He stepped closer, crowding her back against the sliding door. "An athlete, an attorney." Reaching out, he brushed back a lock of her hair. "A model."

She forced herself to remain where she was. Though she knew she should retreat, she wanted to advance, to skim her fingers along the strength of his jaw, to touch her lips to his. It was disgusting, really. "I don't want to be a model," she murmured.

"Then it'd sure make my life a hell of a bunch easier if you didn't look like one."

There was exasperation in his tone. She couldn't help but be thrilled by it, though she tried not to be.

"I was meant to be in law enforcement," she said. "It's in my blood."

"And what about your social life? Have you got one of those?"

His hand was still on her hair. It seemed she could feel the heat of his fingers all the way to her bones. "Not with you," she murmured.

He didn't move. "You know, there have been a few women in my past who haven't found me completely repulsive. Just my luck you'd be in the other party."

She was tempted to laugh out loud, but controlled herself. "Fishing for compliments again, Fox?"

"Just whining about the injustices of life. Unrequited...lust...and all that."

"I'm not the lusty type."

"You sure?"

She didn't answer. "This is my job. I need to do it."

"No, you don't. I could hire someone else, and we could..." He paused, his maple syrup eyes earnest. "Regardless of what you think of me, I could take care of you."

She was one weak puppy. Because despite all her training, all her struggles, all her solemn vows to herself, she suddenly wanted nothing more than to be taken care of by Nathan Fox, to laugh at his jokes and share in his days and let the barriers crumble between them. But she pushed those mushy thoughts out of her head.

"Men have been trying to take care of me all my life," she whispered.

"You can't blame us for being attracted to you."

"It's not because they were attracted," she said. "It was because they thought I couldn't do it myself."

"I guarantee Tyrel would tell you differently."

"Tyrel isn't my brother," she said.

His eyebrows popped up. "Your brother wants to take care of you?"

"They promised Daddy," she said, then snapped her mouth shut and silently reprimanded herself.

"And you have to prove something to them," he said, his tone definite.

Damn her big mouth. "It's just my job. That's all."

His fingers brushed her neck as he swept her hair behind her shoulder. "You don't have to prove anything to *me*, O'Shay."

"I'm not trying to prove anything, Fox. I'm just trying to keep you alive."

"I am alive," he said, and leaning forward, he kissed her.

The heat of his lips seared her senses to ashes. His hand scooped behind her neck, pulling her closer. She bunched her hands in the wear-softened cotton of his shirt, but it seemed she was holding him close instead of pushing him away.

His hand slid down her back. She released his shirt and clasped his forearms. She meant to retreat, but the muscles beneath her fingers were corded and alluring.

His tongue touched her lips. Her hands fell from his arms only to find themselves clasped in his shirt again. But this time they were pulling the garment up, restlessly reaching for more, until finally they fell on the tight, warm skin of his back.

The muscles flexed beneath her hands, alive and strong and warm, begging for more exposure. She skimmed her fingers along his sides to his abdomen and heard the rasp of his excitement against her lips.

That was her undoing. Desperately needing more, she fumbled with his buttons. He wrenched back for a moment, all but ripped the shirt from his body and tossed it to the bed.

In a moment his arms were around her again, and now she could feel the overwhelming strength of his torso against her. His arms, strong and warm and eager, encircled her waist, and through the faded fabric of his jeans and her shorts, she could feel the heat of his arousal.

Her hands skimmed downward, touched his waistband and rushed lower, over the hard curve of his buttocks.

He pulled her closer until she was straddling his thigh. He kissed her throat, his lips hot and demanding and hungry. She arched into him, breathing hard as his kisses dipped lower.

Blood pounded in her ears. Her skin burned where he touched her. His kisses slipped onto the high portion of her breasts, and suddenly his tongue found her nipple through her shirt.

Blood rushed to a thousand unsuspecting places. She heard herself gasp. But the sound seemed to come from far away, and then, like an overcooked noodle, she suddenly went limp.

"O'Shay?"

She heard his voice and tried to rouse herself, but everything seemed vague and foggy as she slumped in his arms.

"O'Shay! Geez!" he said and half carried, half dragged her to bed.

It felt soft and unsubstantial beneath her back. And the ceiling, when she looked up, seemed to waver slightly.

"You okay?"

"Yeah." Her voice sounded funny. "Yeah, I'm fine. Does your ceiling always wiggle like that?"

"Stay right there. I'll get you something."

He was back in a moment. She felt the mattress dip as he settled onto it. "Drink this."

"I'm fine."

"Yeah. Drink it," he said, propping her up slightly.

She took a sip of orange juice, waited a second, then took another. He eased her back to the mattress.

The world stabilized a little. She managed to focus on his face.

"What happened?" he asked.

"I don't know." She still felt as if she were in another dimension.

"Have you fainted before?"

"I didn't faint." She was suddenly, and quite forcefully, offended. "I'm a bodyguard. Bodyguards don't faint."

He remained silent for a moment. "Okay. Have you fallen asleep while standing up before?"

She snorted and tried to sit up. He pushed her back down and stared at her from inches away.

His chest was still bare. Brenna noticed that with only slight heart palpitations and a little hyperventilating. She forced her gaze away.

The silence was heavy, his attention impossible to ignore. She turned her eyes back to his, and noticed with scathing heat that he was grinning.

"I'm flattered," he said.

For a moment she couldn't talk, then, "Get off me," she said, pushing him away.

He didn't budge an inch. In fact, all she achieved was to press her palm against the heat of his mounded chest. Blood started pounding again in unlikely places. She yanked her hand away.

"You like me," he said.

"Get the hell off me."

His grin increased. "Why didn't you say so?"

"Get off me, you big lug!" she demanded, and used her

knee to pry him away from her. In a moment she had gained enough space to sit up.

He lay on his side, propped up on his elbow, with that infuriating grin still plastered on his face.

"It's not you!" she snapped.

"It's either me or you're pregnant," he said and eyed her belly.

She snorted. "I'd *rather* be pregnant," she said, and reached for the orange juice he'd left on the nightstand.

"But you're not," he said.

"Of course I'm not. I'm just..." So embarrassed she'd like to crawl under the bed. It was true, she didn't have a lot of experience with men, but this was ridiculous. So what if he was Nathan Fox? So what if he was famous worldwide, deadly charming, and so good-looking it made her teeth ache? "My blood sugar's a little low. That's all."

"Really?" His grin broadened, plainly indicating he didn't believe a word of it. "Better drink up then."

She did so, though it pained her to take his suggestion. Then she thumped the glass back onto his nightstand. "I'll see you back to the hotel, Fox," she said, preparing to rise.

He snagged her arm. "We could stay here. I'm willing to share my bed."

She glared at him. "We could eat live slugs too, but I'd rather not."

"You like me, B. T. O'Shay. Don't you make me kiss you to prove it," he warned.

She felt her hair go limp as she crouched back into the pillows.

He skimmed his fingers up her bare calf.

"I do not like you," she managed, but her words were whispered.

"Then you lust after me." His fingers did demonic things to her calf. "I think I like that even better."

She knocked his hand away from her leg. "Don't embarrass yourself, Fox," she said and rose snappily to her feet.

The world spun in a sudden downward spiral. She dipped with it, slumping to the bed, but her thighs never touched the mattress. Instead, she was cuddled suddenly and firmly onto Nathan's lap.

She refused to look at his grinning face, but when he spoke there was no sound of laughter in his voice.

"You all right?"

"Yeah."

"I'm going to take you to the hospital."

"The hospital!" She tried to rise, but he held her in a no-nonsense way, easily keeping her where she was. "Don't be ridiculous. I'm fine."

"Has this happened before?" His lips were very close to her ear. She felt her skin tingle beneath the warmth of his breath.

"No." Actually, it had, but not since her mother's funeral, when she'd neglected to eat for days. She squirmed a little now, feeling foolishly like a little kid.

"What'd you eat today?"

She tried a laugh. But he was so close to her, surrounding her really. And there was so much skin, all of it warm and touchable and firm. She wriggled a little, trying not to touch anything she shouldn't.

"I probably haven't eaten enough."

"Probably not," he said. "What would you like?"

Him. Naked. Preferably on his back. With his...

"O'Shay?"

"What!" She jumped at the sound of his voice and thought he paled just a little.

"Listen, sweetheart," he said, his voice rusty. "You'd be doing us both a favor if you'd quit wiggling around."

She stared at him for a split second before his meaning became clear. Then she tried to slip off his lap, but he held her firm.

"Just..." He paused, his gaze warm on her face. "Just stay still and let me hold you for a minute, will you?"

She went still.

He smiled. "You can breathe."

She let her breath out in a whoosh. "Listen, Fox, all I want is to do my job."

"That's not all you want."

Brenna closed her eyes, refusing to see his dark eyes, his packed pectorals, his hard-as-shell abdomen. She pressed her fingertips to her eyes and forced herself to think, to be disciplined, to breathe. "I don't deny that you're a good-looking guy. But I'm just... I'm just not interested." As lies went that was one of her poorer ones, as she was no virtuoso.

"Then why did you swoon?"

She swallowed. "A little low on fuel."

"You didn't kiss like you were low on fuel."

"Listen, Fox!" She felt desperate and scared and shaky. And if he didn't let up soon, she was going to tell him the truth—that she couldn't look at him without imagining him naked beneath her with his bulge hard and his eyes soft. There! How professional was that? "I've worked so hard," she whispered, holding onto her discipline by a tattered thread. "You can't believe how hard I've worked and trained and..." Her voice trailed away as she lost herself in his eyes.

"To prove yourself," he murmured.

"Please," she whispered, "don't make this so hard for me."

For a moment she thought he would kiss her. She held her breath, hoping he would and wishing she didn't. But finally, he slipped her onto the bed beside him.

"What do you want?"

Still him. Naked. On his back. With his...

"To eat."

"Oh." It hardly seemed worth blushing, but she did anyway. "I'll eat at the hotel."

"I'll get you something." He rose to his feet.

She rose too, but he pushed her back down.

"Stay. Or I'll kiss you again, and I mean it."

She sat down like a whipped pup.

"That's better. Here." Leaning over, he fluffed the pillows up against the low headboard behind her. She watched his chest dip into view and managed not to drool. "Lie back."

She considered arguing, but just the thought of his kiss

made her a little woozy, so she scrunched back against the pillows and watched him retreat.

He was back in a minute, a plastic sleeve of crackers in his hand. "Eat these until I bring you something better."

"But—"

"All of them."

She scowled, first at the crackers, then at him, but he was already leaving, taking all that bare skin with him. Sighing, she munched on a cracker.

But Nathan was back in a few minutes, bringing her a glass of milk, a carton of raisins, then finally a plate of scrambled eggs.

"There's no toast," he said, seating himself beside her, his abdomen contracting beneath the ungodly width of his belt buckle. "You'll have to make do." He grinned as he handed her the plate. "See, I won't kick you out for eating crackers in bed."

"I'm flattered."

"You should be." She'd gotten back a little of her spunk, he noticed. But she still looked a little peaked. "Eat that."

"How many eggs is this?"

"Six."

"And you expect me to eat them all?"

"Charming as it is that you faint when I kiss you, I like my women a little more lively—conscious anyway."

"I am not your woman."

"You're in my bed."

She snorted and took a bite. Nuf jumped up beside her, his belly scraping the crumpled coverlet as he sniffed out the eggs.

Nathan swiped him gently aside. The cat sat down grumpily to watch from the sidelines.

"What do you think?" Nathan asked, nodding toward the eggs.

"Not bad," she said, but he noticed that she had already taken a second mouthful. Poor little thing. She ate like a sparrow and worked like a dog. And he was beginning to understand why.

"Ever have a man cook breakfast for you before?"

She gave him a sidelong glance. "Listen, Fox, I work for you. Nothing more."

"Never have, huh?" he said, and entwining his fingers behind his head, leaned back against their shared pillows. He was giving her a clear view of his chest and abdomen, which he liked to think were pretty hard, thanks to the damned weights he kept wedged under his bed. And now that he knew she wasn't repulsed by him, which was a shocking relief, he wasn't above showing off a little. She'd said she wasn't good at this sort of thing. But the truth was, her kiss had just about singed his eyebrows. Oh, boy. Maybe all she needed was a little time. He could give her that. He glanced her way and noticed with heart-stopping gratitude that she was staring at him with those sexy, hotter-than-hell eyes of hers. But he had to keep his head, play this smart. "Not even your brothers?"

"What?" She lowered her gaze back to her plate and blushed.

He loved it when she blushed, like the bloom of a prairie flower. But he wouldn't tease her about it just now, no matter how tempting it was. "Your brothers never cooked for you?"

"No."

A short answer, he mused. He stole a cracker from the pack. "They all younger than you?"

"No."

"Who did the cooking?"

"After Momma died?"

He nodded.

"I did." She didn't like to admit it. He could tell.

Nathan rolled over on his side. Propped up on his left elbow, he could watch her face very closely, read each emotion before she could lock it away. "You must not have had much time to play commando with the boys."

"I was Daddy's..."

"What?"

She shrugged. But the movement seemed stiff. "I was Daddy's little gal."

A wealth of meaning behind that statement. He analyzed each possibility carefully before speaking. "Which meant you did all the housework."

Another shrug.

"And you had five brothers who sat around on their backsides and told you what to do."

"It wasn't like that."

Ah, loyalty. It was a charming attribute. Still, he didn't like these brothers one bit, even though Nathan's own tendencies ran toward the piggish side.

"They began working full-time as soon as they could and started bringing home wages."

"At twelve years old?"

"Don't be silly."

But *she* had worked at twelve and Nathan seriously doubted if wages were involved. Surely that could make a woman hate the jobs generally thought of as feminine. "So do you see your brothers much?"

She gave him another sidelong glance. "I'm awful busy. Traveling and whatnot."

"As a bodyguard."

"Yeah."

"And what do *they* do?"

Turning abruptly away from him, she set the plate on the nightstand. "It's getting late."

"Geez, O'Shay," he said, catching her arm. "You're as jumpy as a mustang. Relax."

She settled tentatively back against the pillows.

"What do your brothers do?"

"One's in the Navy. Two are firefighters, and two are in the police force." Fiddling with a loose thread in the coverlet, she turned her gaze to the overstuffed cat. "Why Nuf?"

"Huh?"

"Why do you call him Nuf?"

"Paul found him a couple years ago when we were touring up north. He was half-froze and all starved. Ate like a horse. The boys started calling him NF." She'd turned her gaze to watch his face. He shrugged. "Short for Nate Fox. Pretty soon they just called him Nuf. They seem to think he personifies the real me." She still stared at him. "Fat, lazy and kind of cocky," he said, answering her unspoken question. "Where do your brothers live?"

"We have to get back to the hotel."

"Not going back to the hotel," Nathan said.

She spun on him like a top at full tilt. "What?"

"Nope." He tried not to grin, but it was pretty much hopeless. "I'm staying here tonight."

"You can't stay here." The look in her eyes could be described as nothing but panicked.

"Why not?"

"Because the cat's not neutered."

Nathan stared at her for a moment, then threw back his head and laughed out loud. "You don't have to worry," he said finally. "I'm housebroke."

"It's not the house I'm worried about."

He chuckled. "You'll be safe."

"Sarge'll worry."

"You think so?"

"Definitely."

"Then I'll call him," Nate said, and rising to all fours, crawled past her to pick up the phone. It took him a minute to get the number and connect with the correct room. Twisting slightly, he sat down, letting one thigh droop over her feet where they rested on the bed. The contact with her toes was nearly more than he could handle, but he smiled, trying to look casual.

"Sarge," he said when the manager answered. "I'm sleeping on the bus tonight. Yeah. She's here. Okay. Yeah. Tomorrow morning. Ten o'clock." He hung up. "There. That's taken care of. We can get some sleep now." He stretched out where he was so that his abdomen was pressed against her bare leg.

She jerked it away as if burned. "We can't both sleep here!"

"I'm just trying to make your job easier."

She gave him a look.

"You gotta guard me, right? And you're not real steady on your feet. But if we're right here together…" He shrugged and reached for his belt.

"What are you doing?" Her voice had pitched up to a squeak.

"Can't sleep in my jeans."

"Sweet Mary!" she said and jerked away, but he caught her arm with a chuckle.

Their gazes caught only inches apart.

"You stay here. I'll sleep on the couch." Dropping her arm, he slipped off the bed, and although he knew he should retreat, he couldn't resist just one more touch.

Gently, he cupped her cheek with his hand. For just an instant, her eyes fell closed. There was nothing he could do but kiss her. Her lips were warm and soft against his, and the tiniest whimper escaped.

It was that whimper that made him draw back, because if he was going to win this battle, he'd have to fight smart.

Her eyes were as big and bright as castanets when he drew away, and beneath his hand, he felt her tremble.

He smiled, leaned forward and tenderly kissed her cheek. "I like you too, O'Shay," he said, and using every bit of self-control he'd thought he didn't have, he turned and walked out.

10

"HOW YOU FEELING?"

Brenna opened her eyes, and there, sitting on the bed next to her was Adonis, unshaven, rumpled by sleep, and so handsome it nearly made her drool.

No wait. She was drooling. Ohhh! She snapped her mouth closed and sat up.

The events of the night before rushed back to her. "What time is it?"

"'Bout seven. I made some breakfast."

She saw now that he had a plate of pancakes in his hand. "Listen, Fox—"

"Don't want to hear it," he said. "I can't have my bodyguard passing out on me. Who'd protect me? Here. Eat this." He handed her the plate, then lifted the syrup from beside her spare contact case.

"How long have you been in here?"

He shrugged. "I don't know. Ten minutes maybe."

She winced at the thought. "Was I drooling?"

He laughed. The sound did bad things to her insides. "Geez, O'Shay, you're so vain. You're my bodyguard, remember? A strictly professional relationship. Hurry up. Eat. I want to take you dancing. I mean—" he grinned "—running."

THE DAYS FLEW BY as did the miles. Oklahoma, Kansas, Colorado, all blurred together with the performances and the duties and the fans.

Brenna did her job as she had from the first day, mulling over the letters, analyzing the threats. Who was sending them? Someone who knew him well. But with the kind of publicity he generated, that could be anyone.

She worked hard and late, and although her schedule never let up, something was different now. Instead of standing in her way at every turn, Nathan seemed to be accepting her presence, informing her when he was going out, consulting about risks, actually helping her do her job.

And although she was still nervous about her role, she would have to say she did her job well. Even the road crew mentioned the difference her presence made. The crowds were more manageable, the performances ran smoother.

They pulled into Omaha on a late afternoon in July. Brenna saw to the usual details while keeping an eye on Nathan as he rehearsed. Afterward Sarge mounted the stage, his boxy body rolling along, his clipboard hugged against his hip.

"So, Fox, you got a date for tonight?"

"Tonight?" Nathan set his guitar aside. The music ceased. Brenna pulled herself from the emotions with an effort. Eventually, she would get used to it, she thought.

"Dinner with me and Shauna. Remember?"

"Oh, yeah. I'm set. Seven o'clock, right?"

"You're not going to try to slime out of this, are you?"

"No. I'm planning on it. Shauna coming here?"

"Yeah. We'll pick you up at your room."

"Uh-huh." Nathan turned to fiddle with a mike.

"She's been planning this a long time. You'll be there, right?" Sarge asked, scowling.

"You think I'm going to be abducted by aliens or something?"

Sarge ignored the joke. "She wants to see you. Make amends."

"There's no amending necessary," Nate said. "I told her that."

"Well, she thinks there is."

"Why don't the two of you just go out? You haven't seen her in months."

"Don't be an ass, Fox," Sarge said. "We'll make it a foursome."

"Sure," Nathan said.

Sarge turned with a grunt. Nathan lifted his gaze, and Brenna, caught breathless and staring, tried to pull away.

"Ms. O'Shay?" someone said from behind.

"Yes?" She turned with abject appreciation for the interruption.

"I got some questions about tomorrow night's performance," said the coliseum's manager, and she pinned her attention on work.

The day was slow and long, and though Brenna berated herself a hundred times, the thought of Nate's conversation with Sarge made her crazy. Who was Fox seeing tonight? How long had he had it planned? And how the hell was she supposed to keep from strangling his date?

Regardless of the turmoil inside her, Brenna managed to hide her feelings and maintain her professionalism.

That evening, she let Nathan open his own hotel room door, but insisted on stepping inside first to make sure all was safe.

"No boogies?" he asked.

She made a face and he grinned.

"S'pose you heard that I'm having dinner with Sarge and Shauna," he said.

She nodded, although she wanted mostly to hide under her bed.

"I really think I'll be safe. Sarge's scowl is pretty much enough to scare off anyone. Why don't you skip this little shindig?"

Because she couldn't bear to leave him alone with another woman, especially now that she knew he wanted her to. But she couldn't bear to be there watching him either. She tamped down all the inappropriate feelings and tried for professionalism.

"Who's your date?"

He raised his brows at her. "Why do you want to know?"

"I'm wondering if she's the type to write nasty letters."

"She may have plans for the night. But I'm sure they don't include murder."

He grinned. She ignored it as best she could. "How long have you known her?"

"Just a couple of months. But we got to know each other *real* well right off the bat."

So he'd had sex with her. Something twisted in Brenna's stomach, but she refused to let her feelings show.

"I'll be safe as a babe in his momma's arms," he said.

In her arms...the image tormented her. Maybe she shouldn't accompany them, she thought. But that was the coward's way, she realized suddenly. "I think I'd best come along. I'll be careful not to cramp your style," she said. It sounded a bit more stiff than she had intended.

Nathan shrugged as if unconcerned either way. "It's up to you. But Shauna's got rich taste. You might want to dress up a little."

"I'll try not to embarrass you." Catty. She wanted to draw back the words. But he only smiled.

"See you at seven then," he said.

BUT AT 6:45 BRENNA WAS still in her underwear, her hands clasped in front of her as she agonized over what to wear. Dress up a little, he'd said. But why? So that she wouldn't embarrass herself, or so that *he* wouldn't be embarrassed by *her?*

She dropped her forehead against the closet door. What was wrong with her? Of course he was going to date. He was a healthy, famous, gorgeous, tantalizing—

Shut up, shut up, shut up, she told her mind and made one quick circle around her dressing room before returning to the closet to stare dismally at the limited number of clothes. She'd chosen a wardrobe that looked professional while not looking stiff. But now it seemed pathetically lacking. Maybe she should have purchased something better. Something with sequins, showing a little cleavage, a bit of—

What the hell was wrong with her? she wondered, and snatched a black jumpsuit from its hanger. Ten minutes later, she quit wringing her hands long enough to knock on Nathan's door.

"O'Shay?" he called.

"Yeah."

"Come on in."

She slid her key into the lock and stepped into his sitting room.

"Is it seven already?"

"Almost," she said, trying to sound casual as she glanced about. But if his date had already arrived she was not in the sitting room. Oh God, if they were making out or something, she was going to jump out the window.

"You've really gotta get over being so damn punctual," Fox called from his bedroom.

"I'll see what I can do," she said and tried to peek into his room, but just then she heard him approach and ducked back near an upholstered chair to gaze blindly at a picture on the wall.

In a moment he was in the doorway. She could feel his presence without turning around.

"Could you throw me that bag by the door?" he asked.

"Sure." She turned to do just that, but stopped short. Her jaw dropped as she stared at him. "You're, umm…" Oh, boy. She was in big trouble, because all her blood had suddenly drained from her brain into parts that hadn't gotten a lot of attention for, say…oh…her entire life. "You're not dressed."

He grinned, buck naked but for a towel wrapped around his waist. "Yeah, I know. There was a show on about dolphins. Sucked me right in. Did you know they're considered one of God's most amorous creatures?"

"No." His hair was still wet. It was slicked back and dripped onto his shoulders. One bead rolled down the taut muscle of his deltoid before sliding languidly along his pectoral and past his taut, left nipple. Brenna swallowed. "No, I didn't."

"Yeah," he said. "You gonna throw me that bag?"

"Oh!" She nearly jumped. "Yeah." Rushing over to the

plastic bag by the door, she prepared to actually throw it, but it was filled with small cans and tubes, and wasn't the type of thing one would go tossing about, so she took a fortifying breath and made the long walk across the sitting room to hand it to him.

"Thanks." His tone was casual enough to be nothing more than a chance meeting at a bus stop. Nevertheless, when her fingers brushed his, she couldn't avoid that spark that snapped through her. He turned away. "Make yourself at home. Some of that dolphin show might be on yet."

"Thanks," she said, but she felt no need to learn about sexually overstimulated creatures, because she figured she pretty much had that category sewn up. It was going to be a long night.

He left the doorway, and in a moment she heard his towel drop to the floor, heard the ting of a hanger as he drew out his clothes. Her knees were starting to sweat.

"You didn't see anyone in the hallway, did you? A tall blond woman—looks kind of like Madonna?"

Oh God. Brenna stared down at her plain black jumpsuit and serviceable flats. It was an okay outfit to run down prospective murderers in, but not quite suitable for boosting her ego while she hung out with a country-and-western superstar and his Madonna.

"O'Shay?"

"No. No, I didn't," she said, wanting to weep.

"Well, I suppose they'll be here soon enough." He stepped into the doorway again. She tried to look away, but found herself sadly undisciplined. To her depressed relief, she found that he had his jeans on. They were zipped, though unbuttoned, and he was pulling on a shirt.

She watched his muscles flex from his chest to his sagging belt buckle as he reached up to straighten his collar. There seemed to be a decided lack of oxygen in the room.

"You all right?" he asked. "You look a little pale."

"I'm fine." Breathe. Breathe. Breathe.

"Good, 'cause it's going to be a long night."

No kidding. Why the hell didn't he get those buttons fastened before she passed out?

"You got your Glock with you?"

"Actually, I had to leave—" she began, but a knock at the door interrupted her.

"Excuse me," he said, and shoving his shirt into his jeans, hooked his trademark oversize buckle onto his belt.

He gave her a look over his shoulder and pulled the door open before she had a chance to realize she should have been doing that.

"Shauna," he said. "It's good to see you. Come on in."

A woman stepped inside. Sarge passed her and stepped into the room, but Brenna barely noticed. For she knew instantly that this was the woman Nathan had been asking about. It wasn't his own date who looked like Madonna. It was Shauna Summers. And if Nathan was going to try to outdo this woman with his own, Brenna was in for a seriously depressing evening. Being around one dazzling, six-foot woman dressed in a fringed red evening gown and matching gloves was enough, but being around two might very well kill her.

Was it too late to flush her head down the toilet?

"Nathan." Shauna took both his hands and stared intently into his eyes. Then leaning forward, she kissed him on the cheek. "How are you doing?"

"Oh, I'm surviving," he said, and laughed.

If Brenna wanted to be really catty, she could imagine that Shauna looked disappointed by his lack of mooning over her.

"We ready to go?" Nate asked.

"Sure," Shauna said. When she shrugged, her boobs, big as Florida grapefruit, popped into sight. The toilet called. "How about you, Bradley?" she asked, glancing toward Sarge who stood near the center of the room.

Bradley? The name seemed strangely incongruous for Sarge, who was dressed rather nattily—tweed jacket, stylish brown felt hat and all. Not a clipboard to be seen. He slicked his hair back a mite and returned his hat casually to his head. But Brenna couldn't help noticing that there was a hard glint in his eyes. Maybe he wasn't too fond of having Shauna and Nathan together either.

"What about your date, Fox?" he asked.

Nathan flashed his gaze to Brenna, and in their depths there was a spark of fire-bright trouble. "B.T. was nice enough to consent to come along."

Brenna just barely stopped her eyes from popping out of her face.

Sarge turned his shrewd gaze on her and buttoned his suit jacket. "You surprised me again."

Shauna glanced askance at her date, then back at Brenna as she stepped forward. "You're called B.T.?"

Brenna managed a nod. Shauna held out a gloved hand.

"Nice to meet you. I love your outfit. Jumpsuits never fit me."

That's because her legs were nine feet long and her breasts were five sizes larger than the rest of her body, Brenna reflected unkindly.

"Come on," Sarge said, pulling the door open. "I'm starving."

Brenna tried to get her bearings, but suddenly Nathan was beside her, grinning down into her face with his hand light but firm on her back. "Ready?"

"I thought you had a date," she rasped.

"I do," he said and laughed as he ushered her out the door.

Inside the limousine, Sarge and Shauna kept the conversation rolling, giving Brenna time to think. But she couldn't because Nathan's arm was draped across the back of her seat. True, his fingertips were barely touching her shoulder. But even that was more than her fragile self-control could handle, because she kept imagining his fingers in other places, against her cheek, her collarbone, skimming down the length of her arm. And from there the images deteriorated into down and dirty.

The limo pulled to a stop. The driver got out and opened the first door, but Nathan was already stepping out on the opposite side. Reaching inside, he helped Brenna out.

She should reprimand him, remind him that she was his employee, but as she emerged from the car, he smiled. "You smell great."

A thrill shivered through her, but she scolded herself. She shouldn't have worn perfume.

"You look good in black. Very dramatic."

His hand touched her back again and the thrill turned to a tiny flame. Bad girl.

They were seated almost immediately, the four of them at a high table that overlooked the city.

"Nice place," Sarge said.

"You know me," Shauna said with a laugh. "I appreciate the finer things. Have you been here before, B.T.?"

"No. I've never been to Omaha."

"Oh. I thought you were from here."

"No." She slipped her gaze to Nathan, trying to figure out what to say. Yes, she probably had the right to slap him upside the head, but he was sitting very close. Now and then his knee would touch hers. And somehow the idea of slapping him seemed a thousand light-years away.

"She's from Mississippi," Nate said.

"Oh. How long have you two known each other?"

"Two months," Nathan said. "A little more."

Damn him for that twinkle in his eye. He was enjoying all this. Enjoying that she was put on the spot. Enjoying all of it. But maybe not enjoying it as much as her knee was. Bad, bad knee.

"I'm his bodyguard," Brenna said. The words fell into the room like a half ton of horse manure.

Shauna's bleached brows shot toward her back-combed hairline. Not a soul spoke. Shauna stared at Brenna, then at Nathan, while Sarge kept his narrowed gaze intently on his girlfriend's face.

"I told you that after all them accidents Fox hired a body-guard, sweetheart."

"Yes, but..."

Nathan lifted his water glass. Mischief sparkled in his eyes.

"She probably expected B. T. O'Shay to be...taller," he said.

THE EVENING WENT MORE SMOOTHLY after that. There were no blank silences during the limo ride back to the hotel.

"If you want to come up to my room I'll order up some drinks," Nathan said as they stepped into the lobby.

A trio of young men entered from a side hall. Brenna got a brief flash of white hair and a pimpled expression, before Ian darted back into the hallway, leaving his two roadie companions to stare after him in bewilderment.

"What was that about?" Shauna asked.

Brenna shrugged and tried not to wince.

Nathan chuckled.

"Sure. We'll come up for a couple of drinks," Sarge said, not seeming to notice the exchange.

The elevator ride was relatively quiet. Finally, Nathan slipped his key card into his door and without a pause, allowed Brenna to step in first.

She flipped on the lights and did a quick once-over while they trooped in behind her.

"They're not kidding," Shauna said when she returned. "You really are a bodyguard."

"I really am," Brenna said.

"I've been waiting all night for them to yell, 'Fooled ya'," Shauna admitted.

Brenna laughed. Despite Shauna's bold beauty and expensive tastes, she was hard to hate. But Brenna was willing to work at it. After all, Nathan had once been in love with her. In fact, Brenna had a sinking feeling that he still was.

"What do you want to drink?" Nathan asked.

Shauna and Sarge placed their orders, but Brenna shook her head.

"Disciplined," Shauna said.

"Yeah, but when she lets loose, watch out," Nathan said from close at hand.

It was one of the few references he'd made to her weaknesses since she'd nearly passed out on the bus, and she refused to blush. Unfortunately, her mind and her body were not always in sync, so she turned away while Nathan picked up the phone and called down orders.

A sheet of notepaper lay on the sofa table behind the leather couch. It was probably scribbled lyrics. Nathan was notorious for leaving them everywhere. She hadn't noticed it earlier. Of course, Nathan had been in a towel, and if the hotel had exploded and a thousand pieces of molten lava had rained down on her head, she probably wouldn't have noticed that either. She skimmed the sheet.

Her breath stopped in her throat.

"You sure you don't want anything?" Nathan asked.

She turned stiffly toward him, her heart like a slow dirge in her chest.

"What's wrong?" He dropped the receiver and rushed across the room to her. "Are you dizzy? Sit down."

She shook her head, feeling sick to her stomach. "The letter."

"What?" He was holding her arms and scowled into her face.

"Where'd you get the letter?"

"What—" he began and stopped as he noticed the paper. His hands dropped from her arms and he took an abrupt step toward the table.

"What's the matter?" Sarge stepped up, his expression taut.

"Don't touch anything," Brenna said shortly. "And call the police."

11

"I SHOULDN'T HAVE TOUCHED THE LETTER," Brenna said.

"Don't be so hard on yourself." Nathan watched her carefully. "The police said there weren't any prints except in the corner anyway."

"Where *I* touched it."

"You didn't know."

"I should have." Her voice was ripe with self-incrimination. "How did he get in here?" Suddenly she felt roiling frustration.

"I thought it was a *she*."

"What?"

"You said the letters were from a woman." He dropped into a nearby chair and stretched his legs out in front of him. Geez, it had been one hell of a long day, and he wanted nothing more than to forget the whole mess. "I'd kind of warmed up to the idea, thinking she maybe finds me irresistible."

"It's not funny, Fox."

He grinned a little, because she was so cute, and desirable and real, like apple pie just out of the oven. And he was getting damn tired of acting as if he thought of her on a professional level only. But he was trying to give her time, time to see how right they were together. But, hell, if that didn't work, he was willing to settle for straight lust. He'd thought after that first kiss by his bed that the battle was already won. But damn, this cute little apple pie woman was as stubborn as Moses.

"I didn't say it was funny," he said, still watching her. She looked very tired, and he found he wanted only to take her into his arms and hold her until everything was all right again. "But it's not as serious as you make it sound."

"How do you know?" she asked, rounding on him like a bull out of a chute. "How do you know what this guy intends? Why would he be writing all these letters unless he has something planned?"

"It probably doesn't have anything to do with the other letters. All he said was he was glad I stopped in Omaha."

"What about your weight?"

"He thought I'd lost some weight. So?"

"And he hoped you weren't fretting about something."

"Yeah?"

"He made a reference to your looks and your health. Just like the others. And what would make you fret more than these letters?"

Nathan remained silent for a moment, watching her. "He's trying to scare me."

"Exactly."

"So he just wants to get me riled."

"Maybe," she said softly and closed her eyes to rub them lightly.

She looked frazzled and frustrated. He wanted to kiss her, to tell her everything was all right, that she was the smartest, cutest little bodyguard in the world. But he knew her well enough to realize that he'd better not.

"Sarge sure doesn't think it's just a prank," she said.

In fact, Sarge had asked the police as many questions as O'Shay had, and had insisted they show the note to a handwriting expert. It made Nathan feel rather guilty for sometimes thinking Sarge was jealous of him. But just now assuaging O'Shay's worries was his first concern. "Sarge thinks too much. Always has," he said.

"Shauna doesn't think it's a prank either."

Nathan watched her. If he tried really hard, he could believe he saw some jealousy in her eyes. And why not? Shauna was a beautiful woman. Icy cold, calculating as an assassin and didn't hold a pale candle to O'Shay's earthy allure, but a beautiful woman nevertheless.

"Why do you say that?" he asked, trying to keep the glee out of his tone. Even if she was jealous, it didn't mean she couldn't live without him.

"Didn't you notice? Shauna went as pale as a sheet when she saw the letter. Didn't she know about the threats?"

Nathan shrugged. It came as a mild, but very welcome surprise to find that he didn't give a rat's ass what Shauna Summers thought. "Shauna's a master at theatrics."

"I think she cares about you."

Nathan stood up, intrigued by the intensity of her expression and so hopeful it made his teeth ache. "Funny. That's what I used to think, too. Turns out Shauna only cares about Shauna." He stretched his arms and said quietly, "It's late, O'Shay. And I've got a show tomorrow. How 'bout we get some sleep?"

She let out a heavy sigh and nodded. "Hook the chain behind me, and don't let anyone in until you call me. Promise?"

There was honest worry in her eyes. Why? Because she didn't want to be the one to explain his dead body to Sarge? Or because she cared about him? Suddenly he needed to know, needed to hold her in his arms, needed her to trust him, to spend some time, to talk about herself.

The sad part was, he wasn't above cheating to find out, to keep her close, to hear about her past and, yes, to fan any possible flames that she might have burning for him.

"You're leaving?" he asked softly.

Her eyes were as big as heaven when she stared at him. "I'll be right next door."

A thousand possible pleas went through his mind. None of them sounded very convincing. "I think we'd be safer together." He was careful to keep his expression absolutely sober, though his heart was racing overtime. "It's not that I'm afraid for *myself*." There was nothing like a good denial to make a woman believe the opposite. "But *your* life might be in danger too." He shuffled his feet a little and wished he'd removed his boots so he looked smaller, more boyish.

He thought of sticking out his lower lip, but overacting might well prove to be his downfall.

"I'm sure I'm perfectly safe," she said softly.

"You never know. And if something happened to you because of me I'd never forgive myself." He paused, realizing suddenly that it was true. She'd become part of his life, like the air he breathed. "Stay with me tonight," he said.

"It...it wouldn't be...professional."

"I'll regale you with stories about myself."

She hesitated.

He allowed a corner of a self-effacing grin. "Don't make me say I'm scared, O'Shay."

The shock and sympathy on her face almost made him feel guilty. Almost. But, damn! He'd waited a long time for a woman like her.

"Please?" He said the word softly.

The silence lasted forever.

"I guess I could stay this once."

Yes!

"I'll sleep on the couch."

No!

"Sure," he said, stemming the tide of his impatience. "The couch is fine."

They stared at each other. She cleared her throat. "I'll go change my clothes."

Clothes? As in a clunky old sweat suit or something. He stepped quickly forward and reached for her hand. It felt flower-petal soft and small in his own. "Don't leave." He laughed at himself, for the desire to keep her close at hand was as real as his pathetic tone implied, even though his reasons were somewhat different from what he was telling her. "I know I'm being ridiculous. Probably just overtired. But..." He shrugged, going for that boyish look again. "I can get you something to wear."

"I don't think—"

"Please?" he said again.

She stared at him and Nathan winced. Had he gone too

far with his little-boy act? He almost squirmed beneath her hard gaze.

"All right," she said finally.

"You're a gem. Come on in." He turned toward his bedroom.

She followed slowly and paused at the doorway.

"You can borrow anything you like." He pulled open a drawer. "Shorts, T-shirt, snakeskin boots?"

"I don't think the boots will be necessary."

He turned toward her. She was standing very still, as fresh and lovely as Mother Earth. "You'd look good in snakeskin," he said.

She stiffened. Nathan gave himself a mental slap and turned back to hide his expression in the drawer. Slowly, slowly. Don't scare her off. "Long sleeves or short?" he asked, trying to fill the uncomfortable silence before she knew there was one. He heard her shuffle her feet in the doorway.

"Long, I guess."

"Long it is." He pulled out a flannel shirt. He'd worn it a hundred times if he'd worn it once and it was as soft as chamois. "Here you go." He held it out to her.

She took a step into the room but raised her brows as she did so. "I think I'm going to need a little more than that."

"Oh, yeah, modesty," he said, and flipping through the pile of clothes again, came up with a pair of silk boxers. They were black with little red foxes printed on them, one of the less ridiculous gifts his road crew had given him over the years.

She reached dubiously for his offering. Their fingers brushed. Nathan felt the impact like the slug of a forty-five. He rose to his feet, drawn hopelessly toward her.

"I...um..." She took a cautious step back. "I better get changed."

"Oh. Yeah. Just... You stay here. I'll..." He motioned vaguely toward nowhere. "I'll brush my teeth," he said, and pushed himself out the door.

But once outside, he stood still and listened, listened for

the sound of her zipper, the drop of her shoes, and grinned. Then, remembering to play smart, he padded away.

It was difficult to tell exactly how long to wait before he reentered his bedroom. He didn't want to appear too early and scare her off. So he counted to twenty, tossed his jacket on the couch, unbuttoned his shirt so she could see his scar, and paced once around the sitting room. Then he hurried back to the bedroom door.

One quick knock with his knuckles. "O'Shay?"

"Yeah?"

"You decent? I forgot my toothpaste."

"Um, yeah. I guess."

Oh God! She wasn't sure. That could only be a good sign, he thought, and cracked the door. "Sorry," he said and stepped inside.

She was wearing his flannel shirt. The sleeves drooped past her fingertips and the green plaid made her eyes seem to swallow her face. Beneath its hem, her legs were bare and smooth.

He tried to control his breathing. But a little demon had taken control of his lungs, squeezing them like a bellows. She stood beside the bed where she'd neatly piled her clothes, shoes on top, and blinked at him like a fawn ready to scamper for cover.

"Well..." He moved past her to the case beside the bed, but the space was narrow, and their arms brushed. He remembered to breathe and move on. Dipping his hand into his case, he found his toothpaste and straightened. He knew he shouldn't stare at her. He knew he shouldn't. And yet... "Lucky shirt," he said softly.

Her lips parted slightly, and for a second he thought she might come to him, but in a moment her fists tensed.

"Sorry," he said quickly and took a step toward her. "I...uh...I'd like to thank you."

She remained where she was. It was funny—she could be as fierce as a badger in a pinch, or she could be like this, all feathery softness and eyes as big as the sky.

"I'm just doing my job," she said.

He almost smiled, because her words were so adorable when she was standing there in his oversized shirt and silk boxer shorts.

"This may be above and beyond the call of duty," he said and grinned a little.

The corner of a smile tilted her lips.

He took two more steps nearer and now, because he couldn't help himself, he touched her face. "I won't forget it," he murmured. "Not for as long as I live." Her hair was soft, conjuring up a hundred tactile images in his mind.

"When I was a boy we used to go trail riding every fall. Sometimes I'd find milkweed pods and break them open. The down was as soft as silk. I'd slide my fingers through it and feed it to the wind as I rode along." He smoothed her hair gently back, skimming his fingers along her jaw and across her ear. "Your hair feels like that. Like freedom and wind and homespun dreams."

Her shiver was almost imperceptible, but he felt it nevertheless. There was nothing he could do but touch his lips to hers. The caress was like magic, like the spark of a firefly, bright as hope, warm as summer. But he didn't rush it, didn't dare.

And she came to him. Her lips moved gently against his, and her hand, narrow and delicate and cautious as a fawn, slipped beneath his shirt. He almost moaned against the ecstasy of that simple touch, almost lifted her in his arms and carried her to bed. But he did not. Instead, he let her lead the way.

Their kiss deepened, her hand slipped sideways, rippling across his abdomen. He pulled back slightly and sucked in his breath, forcing himself to remain still beneath her tentative touch. Her fingertips were like magic, setting him ablaze as they trailed upward, exploring, touching, brushing over his pectoral, his nipple. He gritted his teeth at the fierce sensations. Her hand cupped his chest, trailed along the muscle, taut with tension, beneath his arm and then around to his back.

Nathan could wait no longer. Gently brushing aside her

collar, he kissed her throat. The softness of her skin was like Scotch, hot, rich, and intoxicating. He moved lower. Her top button sighed open and he kissed her there. Another button, another kiss, at the top of her breast this time.

She gasped, but didn't move, one fist clasped tight in his shirt, the other lying flat against his burning side. "I've got to go."

"Too fast." He felt taut with desire and the burning need for discipline. "Sorry. I'm doing my best..." He fought to control his breathing. "Trying not to scare you."

"What?" The word was a whisper against his cheek.

He snapped his gaze to hers, knowing immediately that he'd made a mistake. "I mean, I'm sorry I was scared. It's not very...macho."

"That's not what you said. You said you're trying not to scare me."

Oh damn! "I'm trying not to *be* scared," he said. "Having you here makes me forget—" he scanned for possibilities "—forget that someone broke into the sanctity of my room. Dared—"

"You were never scared," she said, her tone tight.

Damn! It was the word sanctity that had given him away. It was too big for a simple guy like him. Cowboys should stick to words like "shucks" and "dang." "I was scared. I *am* scared," he countered. And it was true. He was afraid she'd never let him near her. Never let him past her guard, into her trust, into her heart.

"Tell me the truth," she rasped.

"Well..."

"You weren't!" she said, pushing him away. "It's all a game to you. Nathan Fox, superstar—lionized, idolized, invincible. You don't believe you need a bodyguard, and even if you did, you wouldn't believe in me. You never did."

"That's not true," he said, stepping toward her, hand outstretched.

She slapped it away, stirring frustration up inside him.

"Yes, it is. You just think I'm a...*woman!*"

He raised his brows at her, trying to control his own latent temper, but frustration was taking its toll, especially when he was watching her breasts rise and fall beneath the soft fabric of his shirt. And in the sharp V where he'd released the buttons, he could see the soft curves of her breasts. "You're not a woman?" he asked, trying to lighten the mood.

She ground her teeth and grabbed her clothes from the bed.

"I've got to admit you had me fooled," he said.

She growled something unintelligible and threw a shoe at him.

He ducked. It glanced off his shoulder.

"I'm leaving!" she snarled and stormed toward the door.

He trailed after her, trying to think of something clever to say, but "I'm sorry" seemed pathetically weak, and "Please stay" seemed dangerous. So he kept silent, but in a moment she stopped on her own and pivoted wildly toward him.

"No, I'm not leaving," she said. "It'd be just like you to think it funny to go and get yourself killed. And I'm too good a bodyguard to let that happen. I'm sleeping on the couch. And if you so much as touch my toe—" She stabbed a finger at him. It barely reached past the plaid cuff. "They'll have to carry you to the stage on a gurney. You understand me?"

He should keep his mouth shut, march into his bedroom and stay there like a whipped cur. But his temper drained away in the face of her delectable cuteness.

"I know it's a cliché, but you really are—" he began.

"If you say I'm beautiful when I'm angry, I'm going to beat you to death with my shoe!"

"Oh. Well..." He backed toward the door, trying to contain a smile. "Good night then." Slipping inside, he pushed the door nearly closed, then peeked past the edge. "But you really are cute when you're mad," he said and thumped the door shut.

Her shoe hit it dead center.

Yep, Nathan thought from the safe side. He'd handled that pretty damn well.

12

BRENNA TOSSED AND TURNED that night, but there was no need, for no one disturbed her. By the time Nathan stepped out of his room in the morning, she was fully dressed and emotionally armed. Or as armed as she could be against his sleepy allure.

He made no reference to the night before, neither to the letter nor to his own duplicitous behavior. Instead, he shifted back into casual banter, as if she were one of the boys again.

They went running. She followed him down the streets of Omaha and watched his back. He asked her to join him for breakfast. She refused, and he refused to allow her to stand by his table like a proper guard, so she sat across from him and watched him eat. Late that morning, he ordered a car around and they drove to the nearest Western store, where he stood for an hour and tried on hats and shirts and jeans, and asked her opinion about the fit of each. So she watched his…well, pretty much everything. In the end, he purchased a Western cut jacket he hadn't even tried on and insisted on buying her a pair of snakeskin boots. She refused, of course, but he swiped away her objections and kneeling down in front of her, insisted on helping her try them on.

It was a bad idea, because her legs were one of the few places that weren't already tingling from watching his everything all day. Refusing to sit down, she stared down at his bent back, watching his cotton shirt stretch tight over his flexing muscles and his tight backside press against the seams of his jeans.

By five o'clock that night, Brenna was cranked tighter than The Fox's guitar strings. She was primed for trouble, almost hoping for it, but Nathan's performance went without a hitch. Still, revved with energy, she made certain she was everywhere at once, checking everything from the electrical wiring to the security systems, and interrogating everyone but Nuf if he so much as crossed Nathan's path.

Outside, it was raining hard and steady. Lightning crashed, making her jumpy and tense.

But finally, she heard the beginning of The Cowboys' final song. It was a soft, romantic number. She felt herself lulled by the magic of his music, remembering his touch, the look in his eyes, the...

No. Damn it! He didn't believe in her. Never believed in her. Thought she was a silly girl pretending she was a man, and she—

"Brenna."

She jumped at the sound of her name.

"Patrick!" Her brother's dark hair was dripping wet, his expression somber. "What are you doing here?"

He scowled. "You know exactly what I'm doing here. The question is, what the hell are you doing here, girl?"

She straightened her back slightly. Being called "girl" was only slightly preferable to being called "butch." "I'm doing a job, Patrick," she said, keeping her tone even. "Go away."

He had always had a quick temper. It shone in his eyes now. "You're being idiotic, is what you're doing," he said. "I came to bring you home."

The anger boiled higher. "What?"

"Listen, maybe you don't know it, but we've been worried terrible about you, and I'm not gonna let you get yourself killed because of some wild notion you got—"

"Wild notion?"

"Yeah."

"Wild notion? Listen here, Patrick Kevin O'Shay, I am not going back with you. So you can just march back to—"

"I'm not marching anywhere without you. Shamus said to bring you home and that's just what I'm gonna do," he said and grabbed her arm.

She struck without thinking, jabbing him one hard strike to the xiphoid process. He stumbled back.

Brenna winced, but her back was still up. "Now you go home, Patrick," she ordered him, knowing Nathan would soon be exiting the stage. "Go home and leave me alone."

She turned away, but in that moment, he launched toward her from a bent position. She heard him coming and swung around, but he was already upon her. Her elbow hit him square in the nose. He skipped to a halt, but his shoes were wet, and the floor slippery. His feet slid out from under him. His arms windmilled for an abbreviated second, and then he fell, flat on his back on the concrete floor.

The back of his head hit an instant later. He lay there still and limp.

Brenna gasped and rushed up to him. But when she dared touched her fingers to his throat, she found his heartbeat normal and his breathing regular.

"Jesus, O'Shay, what happened?" asked Fry, the first to exit the stage.

Brenna rose, bit her lip, and tried not to wince as the other musicians gathered behind him.

"He refused to leave," she said lamely.

"Leave where?"

"The backstage. No one's allowed backstage. You know that." Her voice was getting stronger, and a good thing too, because it looked as if Patrick was beginning to come to.

"Maybe he's the guy who's been writing the letters," Mueller suggested.

"No!" Brenna's voice sounded a bit panicked to her own ears. Her brothers might be an overbearing clan of Neanderthals, but it was bad enough she had gotten Brady in trouble. She didn't want to do the same to Patrick. She smoothed out her voice. "He was just a little overzealous."

"He's waking up," Paul said.

Brenna turned her attention to Patrick and realized the drummer was right. "You guys better get out of here," she said.

"Shouldn't we hang around? Make sure he's all right?"

"Go call the paramedics from the bus," Brenna said. "If the media shows up, it's best if you're nowhere in sight."

Talk of the media made the drummer back away with wild eyes. In a moment, the band had disappeared, leaving only Nathan beside her.

"What's going on?" His voice was low.

"I told you. He refused to leave. Said he was looking for a girl." She turned away to find help, but Nathan grabbed her arm.

"And he mistook *you* for one?" he asked wryly.

"No! He grabbed me," she said and tried to yank out of his grasp, but he held on tight and moved in close.

"What? He touched you? Why? Do you know him?"

Anger and concern and frustration shone in his eyes and sounded in his voice. Brenna fell silent, transfixed by the sight.

He blew out a breath and narrowed his eyes as if steadying himself. "You all right?" he asked, his voice softer but still gruff.

For a moment she was lost in his eyes, but she pulled out with an effort. "I can take care of myself, Fox."

He stood unspeaking for an instant, but then he dropped her arm. "Yeah. Who is he?"

"I...I don't know. Just some guy. Probably looking for his girlfriend. Maybe one of the road crew was with her here in town." It was a pathetic cover-up if she'd ever heard one. "You'd better go."

"What happened?" Patrick's voice sounded gravelly, and he didn't try to sit up.

"You fell," Nathan said, stepping forward into Patrick's line of vision. Brenna winced, wanting to snatch him back, but it was too late. "You okay?"

"Feel like I've been kicked by a mule."

"She can act like one," Nathan said, squatting down.

"What?"

"You better lie still. Were you looking for someone?"

Patrick was silent for a moment, then, "Brenna. I think..."

He lifted his head from the floor and tentatively felt the back of his cranium. "Should of known better."

"She your girlfriend?"

"My sister. She—"

"Stand back! Let us get in here," called a paramedic, rushing in.

Nathan moved regretfully aside as the troop circled the downed fellow.

Brenna dared a quick exhalation as orders and questions were thrown at Patrick.

Nathan stepped away from the orderly chaos. "He was looking for his sister," he said.

"Yeah. Guess so."

"Probably had too much to drink."

"Uh-huh."

"You know, he looks a little like that drunk you tangled with in North Carolina. It's not him, is it?"

"No!" Too sharp. She softened her tone. "No. It's not. The other guy was blond. Younger. I, uh…checked into his history after we left Charlotte. He's not the same guy." She shuffled her feet and refused to shift her gaze from his.

"You sure?" He watched her carefully.

"Yeah. Uh-huh. I'm sure."

"Okay. Well, I don't think this guy meant any harm. No need to call the police. Do you think?"

"No." She tried not to say it too quickly. "I think he'll be fine…when he sobers up."

Nathan nodded and turned away, but in a second he glanced sideways toward her. "What was his sister's name?"

"I, um…I don't remember."

"Really?" He put a hand gently to her back as he ushered her through the first door. "You usually have such a good memory."

THEY WERE ON THE ROAD within an hour. Although The Cowboys wouldn't perform for another two days, the band had interviews and personal appearances in Minneapolis on the following day.

Brenna fretted the whole way as a thousand worries tore at her. Okay, so her Neanderthal brothers had been begging to be belted. Still, guilt gnawed at her. But the thing that worried her most was the note found in Nathan's room. How had it gotten there? No one had access to his room. She'd checked with the front desk and made absolutely certain that no other keys had been given out, and that none of the hotel's employees had delivered the note. None had.

It was as if a ghost had walked right through the walls to slap her on the face, to threaten her client. And yet her client seemed unconcerned Brenna realized, glancing over at him where he strummed his guitar and hummed a few bars.

The days passed without incident, and although Brenna wouldn't have thought it possible, Nathan seemed even more relaxed than ever. His performance in Minneapolis was to a sold-out crowd. Everything went like clockwork, and yet Brenna was nervous as she escorted Nathan to his bus.

Atlas was already behind the wheel. From the back of the bus, Nuf gave his grumpy call, but didn't come forward to meet them.

Nathan plopped onto the couch, and Brenna, nervous and fretful, took a seat on the other side of the aisle. Within minutes, they were on their way, but the silence stretched on.

Brenna pulled out her agenda, ready to get to work, but still she could feel Nathan's gaze on her.

"Almost done," he said.

"What?" She looked up abruptly.

"The tour. It's almost over. Two more shows and you can forget all this and go home to Jackson."

Forget it? He must be joking, she thought, but didn't voice the words, though her stomach knotted up like a sailor's line. "And what will you do?"

"Gonna spend some time at home. Relax."

"Relax!" She almost barked the word, then calmed herself and tried again. "Isn't it going to be hard to relax?"

"You forget. I'm a lazy ass by nature."

"And you forget," she said, "someone is threatening your life."

He snorted and shook his head. "So hard up for a job that you have to make a place for yourself, O'Shay?"

She glanced out the window and let the terror roll over her. "What will you do about security?"

"Security?" He laughed. "My ranch is in North Dakota, O'Shay. There isn't exactly a deluge of people there, murderous or otherwise."

"You think no one knows where you live?"

"I told my mother."

She refused to be baited by his stupid sense of humor, and tried to remain calm, to remind herself that it was his life, his decision. "You think the threats will simply cease?"

From the back, Nuf called again, his tone no more soothing than usual.

"Come on up, Fats," Nathan called, then, "No. I don't think the threats will simply cease, because I don't think there were ever any threats."

Frustration felt like a boiling pot inside her. "The letters mean nothing to you?"

He shrugged. "A prank."

"And the blowout? The electrical short?"

"Accidents," Nathan said.

"Sweet Mary!" Brenna jerked to her feet and paced the aisle, trying to calm her nerves, to remember that she was a professional. "What the hell are you trying to do, Fox?"

"What do you mean?" His face was impassive when she looked at him.

"What do I mean?" She snarled the words. "You're not that stupid. No one's that stupid. You've been bombarded by threatening mail and freak accidents. But you act like nothing's happened." She swung suddenly toward him. "Why?"

Nuf cried again.

"Geez, O'Shay, you're taking this way too serious." Nathan's tone was relaxed, but his body seemed tense and stiff when he rose to his feet and pushed past her on his way to his traveling bedroom.

"Too serious?" She turned as he passed her.

He stopped in the doorway for a moment. "Geez, cat, what

have you gotten into this time?'' He disappeared, only to reenter a moment later with the overstuffed cat in his arms. Around Nuf's neck was a plastic six-can carrier. ''You're the most suicidal animal I've ever met,'' he murmured to Nuf.

''There's you,'' Brenna countered irritably.

Nathan snorted. ''When was the last time I got my head caught on a drawer handle?'' he asked, and pried the plastic ring from the cat's neck.

''I haven't been around very long.''

He ruffled the cat's fat head before setting him down and lifting the rings between them. ''You been slogging beer again, O'Shay?''

''No,'' she said, irritated by his refusal to see the truth.

''Then where'd he find the hoops?'' he said, tossing the rings to the table.

Brenna turned away, trying to cool her temper, to think, to give Nathan time to see logic. But he was not a logical man. At best, he was an artist; At worst, a heavy-handed, half-witted barbarian. And if—

Her thoughts stopped abruptly. Where *had* Nuf found the plastic rings? Turning stiffly, she paced to the table and picked up the packing bonds.

''Did you leave this in here?'' she asked Nate.

He shrugged, noncommittal. But her heart refused to slow. Turning, she paced up to the driver. One quick question made her certain Atlas hadn't been sloppy.

Wandering back to her chair, she turned the rings in her hand. Nuf was grumpily licking his ruffled fur back into place. She was probably being silly. Nuf was fine, and he was prone to accidents. Closing her eyes, she blew out a quick breath and tried to relax. But just then her fingers scraped across an indentation in the plastic. Breathlessly she lifted it higher, barely daring to look at it.

But she couldn't delay forever. Her fingers told her the truth, even if her eyes refused to see.

''Nathan.'' Her voice quavered. His eyes narrowed when he looked at her.

''What is it?''

"Was the bus locked?"

"Yeah. Why?"

"Are you sure?"

"Geez, O'Shay, if you're trying to drive me insane you're on the right track. What's the problem?"

"Your initials—" she began, but strangely, she couldn't say the rest.

"What?"

She calmed herself. "Your initials are carved into the plastic."

"What are you talking about?"

"Don't touch it!" It seemed, suddenly, like a live grenade in her hands. "There might be prints."

He leaned toward her to scowl at the plastic, then stare pityingly into her face. "Relax. That's not an *N*. It's an *H*. Or maybe..." He looked at it askance. "Tally marks, fence rails, nothing at all..."

She stared at him, not daring to move, to breathe, or even to talk for a moment. But finally, her heart rate and her muscles relaxed a mite.

"What do you want, Fox?" she asked softly.

He watched her from inches away, saying nothing.

"Do you want me to beg?"

"O'Shay—"

"I will," she said softly, unable to stop the words. "If that's what you want, I will."

"What are you talking about?"

She raised her chin slightly. "Please don't go to North Dakota without a bodyguard." Silence, but for the sound of the wheels on the road beneath them. "Please. If you don't want me, I understand."

"O'Shay—"

"I'll find you someone else. I know a dozen good agencies. I'll call one tonight. I'll—"

He grabbed her arms suddenly, his eyes intense. "You're being ridiculous."

Her eyes filled with tears, though she cursed herself for it. "I can hire my replacement by the weekend."

He dropped her arms. "So you're trying to get out of our deal?"

She stared at him, her throat tight.

He turned stiffly away. "I've been leaving you alone, letting you do your job. What more do you want from me?"

"I want you alive."

"Why? To pay your fee? To give references?"

"Please," she said, barely able to force out that one word. "Don't go without me."

"You *want* to go with me to Five Crow?"

She tried to grin. "I won't eat much."

They stared at each other for a brief eternity.

"Fine," he said finally, nodding jerkily. "Fine. You come then." He jabbed a finger at her. "But you're not going to break my heart."

13

BRENNA COULD FEEL Nathan's excitement. He sat across the aisle from her, staring out the window like a small boy at Christmas. Their bus turned off the tar road and bounced onto gravel. Soft green hills, haloed by the sinking sun, rolled into view.

Finally, the bus pulled to a halt, and Nathan was out the door. Brenna followed more slowly, looking about as she left her home on the road. His house was a low building made of natural logs. Behind that, a cluster of wooden barns hung in a half circle. And past that—the low, craggy hills speckled with bent elder and ash trees. Not another building was in sight. A narrow creek meandered through his property, sparkling like rough gold in the quiet hills. Beside it, a herd of horses grazed, their sleek coats nearly as bright as the rustling water.

A thrill of excitement sparked through Brenna. There was something about this country that spoke to the cowboy in her, to the jewel thief, to the little girl she'd lost long ago. Something that touched her, moved her.

Off to her right, she heard Nathan speak to his driver. There were low murmurs of laughter, and then Atlas's footsteps moving away.

Brenna glanced toward Nathan. He stood with his back to the bus, looking out over his land, oblivious to all else. She watched him breathlessly. His emotions, always evident on his face, were even clearer than usual. His love for this land was written in his eyes. And suddenly she wanted to stay here forever, to dip her toes into the water, to lie back on the green grass and learn all there was to know about Nathan the Fox.

He glanced toward her. Brenna turned abruptly away. Scowling at her own foolish thoughts, she hurried back to the bus, reminding herself the whole while that she was here to guard him. Nothing else.

She diligently remembered that when he showed her to her room, a cozy little nook overlooking the south pastures.

She remembered when he gave her a tour of his sprawling, pine-paneled home. And later, when they moved Nuf from the bus to the house, her mission ran through her mind like a litany. Keep him safe. Keep him safe. Don't get involved.

He made spaghetti sauce for supper and when he touched the wooden spoon to her lips and asked her opinion, she was steely tough, even when his gaze, warm as hazelnut coffee, rested on her face.

Later, she stood beside him at the sink and remembered again. Each time he handed her a wet dish to dry. Each time he shared another little tidbit about himself. Each time he breathed, or smiled, or turned just so, so that she could see his profile, or the tanned width of his wrist, or, God forbid, his butt, tight as a fresh plum in his faded blue jeans.

She held her breath as she stared at it.

"Full moon," he said.

"Huh?" She snapped her gaze back to his face.

"There's a full moon tonight."

"Oh." There were just the two of them, alone in this quiet little house in the hills. Oh, indeed!

"A full moon in a sky as dark as Mississippi mud." He hummed a bar, then grinned at her as he wiped his hands on his jeans. "Bet you've never seen a sky as black as ours."

"I—"

"Come on."

"It'd be better if you didn't go out after dark," she said, trying to draw herself out of his eyes.

But he laughed. "You expect me to stay inside? Really, O'Shay!" He stepped an inch closer. She could feel his masculinity like the undertow of a warm wave. "I thought that's why you were here. To keep me safe."

She swallowed hard, and tried to pull her gaze away. But it was hopeless, because his words of some days before kept running through her mind. "You're not going to break my heart" he'd said. But why? Did he, perhaps, care for her a little? Could it be that she was more than a new and intriguing challenge to him?

"Isn't that right?" he asked softly.

"What?" she breathed.

"Aren't you here just to keep me safe?"

Damn it all! She couldn't remember.

"Tell me now, O'Shay," he said, and gentle as a sigh, he touched her cheek. "'Cause if you've got other reasons I'm ready to launch a full-scale seduction."

Her jaw dropped. And against all odds, she managed to shake her head.

"No what?"

She couldn't remember that either.

"Why are you here?"

Oh! She knew that one. "I'm your bodyguard."

"No other reason?" He smoothed his fingers across her cheek, then ran the flats of his nails along her jawline. Her knees threatened to buckle, tossing her headlong into his arms. That'd be bad. Wouldn't it?

Amazingly, she shook her head again.

He drew his hand abruptly away and shrugged as if her reasons were of no concern to him. "Well, you'd better come out with me then, 'cause my body's definitely going to need guarding out there in the spooky darkness."

She mastered the operation of her knees and managed to accompany him outside. They stepped away from the lights of the house. The night was as still as heaven. In the distance, she heard a cow low.

He led her down to the closest barn and switched on the lights. Rows of stalls marched away from them. They walked down the concrete aisle together. Horses blinked at them from behind their barred doors.

Nathan introduced her to each one, smiling as he made the acquaintances, talking to them, stroking a few, telling her anecdotes and stories and dreams.

Finally, they wandered out the back door and into the pasture. The creek meandered like flowing mercury past their feet. More horses grazed on the hillside. They were indistinct and magical in shades of silver and black.

Hearing their approach, the nearest horse snorted and shied, starting the whole herd running. They flew like a band of thundering ghosts, up the dark hillside, seeming to collide with the moon as they made their fanciful escape.

Brenna stood absolutely still, made breathless by their magnificence. "Beautiful," she breathed.

But Nathan said nothing. She turned toward him and caught the glint of his stare.

"You think so?" he asked softly.

She nodded. Keep him safe. Don't get involved. Pulling her gaze away with an effort, she scanned the hilltop. "Where'd they go?"

He remained silent for a moment. "They've got a couple hundred acres. Want to see?"

She managed a nod and took a step away from him, but he caught her hand. "Creek's deeper than it looks," he said, and bending slightly, swung her into his arms.

"What—"

"Gotta keep my bodyguard dry. What if I get…" He shrugged. She could feel the movement of his chest and arms against her own. The warmth of his body seeped into her soul, making her feel heavy and lost. "What if I get shot or something and you have to run home for help?" His face was inches from hers, so magnificently sculpted it made her want to weep. "Wet feet might slow you down."

That made sense, she thought nonsensically. But not as much sense as the feel of his heart beating slow and steady against her arm, or the sound of his voice, raspy and soft on her cheek.

"O'Shay…" he murmured, his lips inches from hers.

Goose bumps quivered over her at the raspy tone of his voice. The moon grinned down from its lofty height.

Damn her mission. She couldn't resist him any longer. "What?" she breathed.

There was a pause. "Do you ride English or Western?" he asked.

"What?"

He dropped her feet abruptly to the grass. "I'm planning to do a lot of riding," he said, striding off. "I suppose you'll have to come along. Do you go English or Western?"

She stood in the darkness, trying to think, to make her legs hold her weight, to remember, God yes, that she was a professional. And professionals did *not* throw themselves in their employer's arms and beg like a shameless dog to be petted.

BRENNA TRIED TO DO HER JOB. She installed a first-rate security system in Nathan's house and horse barn, ordered a privacy fence and gate put across the front of his property, and, most tantalizingly grueling of all, kept diligently by Nathan's side.

The days passed in sweet torture. Meals with his family, infectious laughter, playing hearts in the evening, touching hands as they traded queens and fives.

But through it all, he seemed oblivious to the feelings that sparked from his fingers to hers, and treated her as nothing more spectacular than a buddy.

August came hot and dry. But Nathan had begun conditioning Lula for the upcoming rodeo and refused to stop because of the heat. Instead, he would work the mare early in the morning or late in the evenings.

Tyrel brought his gelding over a couple times a week and they would rope steers together. Brenna sat in the shade, watching their comradery, listening to their laughter, marveling at the way Nathan turned his head or tossed his lariat, or walked, or breathed...

Sweet Mary, she was sick! She rose to her feet, and paced. The sun was perched just above the western horizon, but the heat was unrelenting. She pulled a few stray hairs away from her neck and hoped for a breeze. There was none.

"Hot?"

She jumped at the sound of Nathan's voice, close enough to whisper in her ear.

He grinned. "I thought you were supposed to be watching me. Boogeymen, you know."

She turned away to watch Tyrel turn his rig onto the road.

"I'm thinking you're probably the only boogeyman that comes this far north." She was irritated, not so much by the heat, but by his placidness. Yes, she wanted...no...*insisted* on a professional relationship. But he didn't have to make it look so easy. Not when just being in the same county as him made her feel itchy and squirmy and hot.

He grinned. "It's cooler up in the hills. Want to go for a ride?"

"On horse?"

He quirked an eyebrow. "What else?"

She hadn't thought of it that way, but now a steamy image of her straddling him sizzled in her mind. "I didn't...I don't..." He was watching her very closely, and there wasn't a single rock nearby large enough to hide under. "Of course you meant on horse."

He watched her for a moment longer, but in the end he chuckled low in his throat in that sexy way he had and led her down to the barn. Once there, he insisted on saddling her horse for her, saying she'd better watch his back—just in case. But somehow her gaze never quite managed to rise that high.

Her mount was a leggy chestnut mare called Boo. Her coat matched Brenna's hair within a shade of perfection. The saddle Brenna settled into was a deep-seated Western model with a rubber-wrapped horn and enough wear to make it fit like a comfortable pair of jeans.

They set off down the gravel road at a jog trot. Memories rushed back at Brenna, the satin stride of a good horse beneath her, the feel of power and freedom and peace. She was glad she hadn't become a jewel thief. It was more fun being a cowboy. She silently laughed at herself and drew a breath deep into her lungs as the sun sank into the mulberry red sky.

"Wow," she said softly.

"Yeah."

She turned toward him, only to find his gaze steady on her face, but he turned away in a moment.

"It's said there's no place that has as many pretty sunsets as the Dakotas."

"Who said that?"

"Me." He grinned. "How do you like Boo?"

"She's a beauty."

"You look good on her."

Brenna lifted her gaze to his and felt the usual flare of desire burn her.

"I mean, in a bodyguard sort of way," he amended, and grinned casually.

Didn't he feel the spark, the desire, the *need?*

"Here." He motioned toward a red panel gate to their left, swung his leg over the cantle and dismounted with poetic, long-legged grace. In a moment, they were through and he was mounted again.

"Cattle trail," he explained, indicating the dirt path that twisted westward. "Okay if we lope?"

She nodded and pushed Boo into a faster gait. Wind caught the mare's mane and Brenna's hair in a wild wave. Exhilaration spurred through them both. They thundered along, following Nate's palomino, skirting bent trees and jagged boulders until the trail dipped dramatically downward.

Nathan slowed Lula, and Brenna followed suit.

The sun had sunk below the horizon. Down in the gorge, it was dusky, with the mist already forming over the creek as the warm air condensed. It seemed magical somehow, quiet and moving and mystical.

Up ahead, there was a splash. Nathan pointed to his left, and Brenna caught a glimpse of a white-tail deer as he leapt from the water and away.

Nate slowed Lula and they rode side by side now, for the cattle trail had divided, granting them each a path.

The creek bank to their left grew steeper, the trails closer together. Nathan's knee brushed Brenna's. She held her breath for a moment, and pushed on until, not far ahead, the gorge flattened and the creek widened.

Cottonwood trees surrounded the small oasis and rustled quietly in the slight breeze. Nathan loosened his reins, letting Lula step into the water. She lowered her head and drank. In a moment Boo did the same while their riders sat in companionable silence, watching the night fall quietly around them.

"So this is why you come back," Brenna said quietly.

Nathan turned toward her. She could feel his attention even before she glanced toward him. "I'd say it kept me sane, if I thought you'd believe it."

She couldn't help but smile. "I never said you were crazy. Irritating maybe." She shrugged. "Egotistical, demented—"

He snorted as he dismounted. "Remind me never to fish for compliments with you."

She laughed as she stepped from the saddle. "All right."

The night went quiet around them again. Boo tugged at her reins, trying to reach the spare, coarse rushes that grew at the water's edge.

"Here." Nathan led the way over to a level grassy spot. Untying a pair of hobbles from behind his saddle, he crouched at Lula's front legs and secured them together. "You can just turn Boo loose. She'll stay with Lu."

"You sure."

"Yeah," he said and slipped his own bridle from the palomino's head.

Brenna did the same and in a moment Nathan was hanging the bridles over a tree branch and they were wandering back to the water's edge. Once there, he paced along an outcropping of shale and finally sat to pull pieces of rock from the ledge and toss them into the lagoon.

Uncertainty stirred through Brenna. Should she sit beside him, stand guard over him, try to—

"See any bad guys?" he asked, glancing up.

She scowled at him.

"Wouldn't I be safer if you were right here beside me? That way," he said, grinning a little, though even in the darkness, it almost looked like he tried not to, "you could shield me with your body should anyone start taking pot-shots."

She deepened her scowl.

"You never know," he said. "Come on."

She searched for some kind of excuse to keep her distance. But other than telling him she absolutely couldn't resist him if she sat that close, she could think of nothing to say, so she wandered over and sat down beside him.

The silence was as heavy as the air around them.

Brenna cleared her throat. "I didn't think it'd get this hot so far up north."

He shrugged, and cocking his leg, pulled off one boot, then the other. "It can, for a month or so."

"Oh." She stared out over the water again. Somewhere near the middle, a fish splashed.

Nathan pulled off his socks, stuck them sloppily into his boots and dropped his feet into the water with a sigh.

Brenna was immediately jealous, but she dared not expose that much skin. It would be far too tempting for her. Silence settled in again.

"Wanna go for a swim?"

She jerked her gaze toward him. "What?"

He grinned at her. "Sure."

"I didn't...I don't have a suit."

He shrugged, looking nonchalant as he casually began to unbutton his shirt. "You got underwear on, don't you?"

She tried to glare at him, but it didn't work very well, because she could see the tight mounds of his pectorals now and momentarily forgot how to pry her gaze from his chest.

"Don't you?" he asked again.

She swallowed.

"I mean, not that I have any objections. Either way, it's okay. There's nobody here but me."

Just him? Like there was anyone else in the world?

"No one'll see." He pulled his shirttail from his jeans. "I mean..." His silver belt buckle fell away with a quick flick of his hand.

He stood up. Her gaze rose with him, pinned to his chest like a needle in a paper donkey's rump. He was beautiful, dark, sculpted, and so unearthly alluring in the pearlescent light.

"You're just one of the boys. Right?" he asked.

She stared. He reached for her hand. She knew that if she had the mind of a mole, she'd run like hell, but somehow, her hand lifted of its own accord and settled into his.

He pulled her to her feet. They were face to face now, and so close she could feel his charisma like the crack of a whip.

"I'm going in," he said softly. "What if there's someone lying in wait for me...lurking under the water, waiting to pull me under?" He moved a scant step closer. "And you're not there to save me?"

She was breathing hard, staring up into his face like a lost puppy, hoping he would release her, praying he wouldn't.

"Will you come?" he whispered.

No. She couldn't. She wouldn't. She shouldn't.

He kissed the corner of her mouth.

"Okay," she whispered and realized suddenly that he had stopped breathing.

She raised her gaze to his and he seemed to jerk back to reality.

"Good." He nodded. "I'll just... Do you need help with your..." He motioned toward his own chest. "Anything."

"I can manage."

He turned away.

Her face was hot and her hands shaky. What had she done? What had she said? What was wrong with—

But suddenly she noticed that he was stepping out of his jeans. His legs were sprinkled with dark hair and as long as forever. She stared, noticing how his white underwear clung like a second skin.

He raised his eyes. Their gazes clashed.

"You're awful slow," he murmured.

For the life of her she couldn't think of a single rejoinder, clever or otherwise. And when he stepped toward her, she found her lips could form no objections, and her legs refused to back away.

"Let me help you with those," he said, and reaching out, gently slipped her buttons from their holes. Her blouse sighed open. She felt the breeze lap her hot body, felt his fingers graze her sensitized skin as he slipped the shirt from her shoulders and let it drop to the ground.

His hands delayed a moment on her shoulders, then slid, slow as sorghum down her arms. She shivered at his touch, and held her breath as his fingers grazed her abdomen to find the snap of her jeans.

In a moment, they were sliding down her legs. She felt his hand, large and strong and hot against her buttocks. Felt his breath against her throat. And against her hip, she felt the hard evidence of his desire.

He pulled his hands away with obvious effort. "Maybe..." His tone was guttural. "Maybe you better do the rest yourself."

She tried to nod, to be casual, professional, nonchalant. Indeed, she may even have had a modicum of success, but her shoes had forgotten her vow of chastity. Firmly stuck in her pant legs, they refused to let her move. Brenna tried to pull her leg out, but it didn't work, and so, with a small gasp of dismay, she fell forward.

Nathan caught her against his chest. They remained as they were for a frozen moment, her leaning against him as if he were a wall, and him standing as still as the damn rock of Gibraltar.

"Or maybe I should help you," he murmured against her cheek, and bending slightly, hooked his arm behind her knees and lifted her into his arms.

She could feel each inhalation he made, each rise and fall of his chest against her bare arm.

"O'Shay." He breathed her name like a prayer, their faces inches apart, their hearts all but joined.

"What?"

"You'd better kick off your shoes. Wouldn't want my bodyguard to drown."

Blushing, she snapped her attention to her feet, and managed to do as directed. In a moment, her shoes lay on the ground and her jeans were willing to follow. More than willing, eager, as if every inch of her wanted to be pressed against him.

"Put me down." She managed the words, though her brain was begging her not to.

"You're..." He was staring into her eyes. "You're the lightest bodyguard I ever had."

"I'm the only bodyguard you've ever had," she murmured, her gaze caught on his.

"Oh yeah." He paused. "So I'd probably feel this way about any of them, huh?"

She swallowed, knowing she shouldn't ask. "How do you feel?" she whispered.

"Light-headed."

"Yeah?"

"'Cause no matter what you say, you feel like a woman to me."

She licked her lips. "Nathan..." She was breathing too fast, and it would be really embarrassing if she passed out again. "I..." She let out a heavy breath and tried again. "I can't deny that I'm...attracted to you."

"But you have," he said.

"What?"

"You have denied it."

"I know. But I...I'm your bodyguard. Your employee." It was a strange thing to say, while being held in his arms, pressed up to his chest like a precious gift. "I'm trying to be professional."

"I think you're professional," he murmured, and kissed the corner of her mouth.

She moaned at the touch of his lips. "Listen, Fox, you know you're sexy."

Another kiss, this time to her throat.

"And gorgeous."

A kiss to her collarbone.

"And seductive and alluring and—"

He kissed her full on the lips.

Fire smoked through her. Her hormones were ringing off the hook. But she pressed her hand to his chest and managed to break off the kiss.

"This is…" She was breathing too damn hard. Unconsciousness mocked her. "This is ridiculous."

He stared at her, his eyes as dark as ebony in his sculpted face.

"I'm not your type. You need someone…" She was trying to think. Really she was. But her entire being was pretty much occupied with other things. "Well…I'm a bodyguard. It's what I've always wanted to be. I'm independent and pushy and… And you…" She was panting slightly. "You're arrogant and old-fashioned and…and we're totally incompatible. So I was thinking." She licked her lips again. "Maybe if we did it, just once, we'd get it out of our systems." She said it in a rush, before her brain knew what her lips had in mind.

"Did it?" he said softly.

"Yeah," she whispered, barely able to force out the word. "I'm sure if we…you know…have sex once…we'll see it's not that big a deal and be able to…forget about it."

He was silent for a short eternity. "You think so?"

She cleared her throat. "I'm sure of it."

Somewhere far away, an owl hooted.

Brenna met his gaze. "So what do you say?" she whispered.

"It's a good plan," he said.

14

BENEATH A BENT CLUSTER OF COTTONWOODS, the sand was as soft as silt.

Nathan lowered Brenna there, then settled on his side to lie down beside her. Darkness had settled in like a downy blanket around them. Overhead, the sky was inky black and studded with a billion stars.

Oh yes, he wanted to make love to her, but if the truth be known, he'd wanted to make love to her since the first moment he saw her surrounded by her beefy-necked colleagues. Even so, her reasons for doing it now seemed too asinine to take advantage of. Ridiculous, ludicrous—

Brenna skimmed her fingers up his abdomen to his chest where she traced the crescent shape of his scar. Lightning followed her path, setting him ablaze.

Okay, her reasons weren't *so* asinine.

She moved closer still. Flesh touched flesh, warmth on warmth. Her thigh brushed his, her arm caressed his chest. Nate's breathing escalated.

All right, there was *some* sense to what she said, he admitted breathlessly.

And then she leaned forward and touched her lips to his in a kiss that seared all coherent thought to ashes.

She had a great plan, a wonderful plan, a *phenomenal* plan, he thought, and wrapping her in his arms, kissed her with all the trembling intensity in his soul. She kissed him back with equal heat, and suddenly he couldn't feel enough, couldn't kiss enough, couldn't see enough. Her bra slipped away from breasts firm and soft and round. Her underpants followed suit, along with his. He kissed her legs, her abdomen, the sweet, tiny dell of her belly button. She writhed beneath him, and the sight of her in the moonlight was like hot magic, sucking him in, pulling him under.

He longed to slip inside of her, to feel her wrapped around him, to quench his feverish desire for her. But he couldn't deny that he wanted so much more, wanted her here beside him...forever. Wanted her spark and her spirit and her wit. So he slowed his movements with Herculean effort, letting his fingers trail a languid path between her breasts, needing to make her want him as he did her. She shivered beneath his touch. He kissed her shoulder, her throat, the shivery sensitive crease of her elbow.

She jerked to a sitting position, breathing hard, her hair like a wild jumble of rubies in the moonlight. Her nipples caressed his chest, nearly stopping his heart, and her lips, only a breath away, were parted and strawberry sweet.

Nathan ran a finger over them, felt her exhalations in small pants, then blazed a languorous path down her throat, along the side of her breast and around her taut waist. Rolling onto his back, he pulled her with him. Her nipples teased his chest, and she straddled him, her sweet bottom settled warm and wet against his own turgid heat.

He moaned at the impact and tried to remain still, to give her time. But she reached back and stroked him.

Nathan sucked air through his teeth, going absolutely rigid, and in that moment, she arched upward and took him inside her. With a keening moan she dropped her head back. The moonlight, soft as fairy dust, glanced off her breasts, and for a moment Nathan was paralyzed by her beauty. But then she moved, squeezing him firmly, and he was carried along in the wave of her momentum.

He pressed into her with a groan of ecstasy and suddenly there was nothing but the soaring search for pleasure. Nothing but the touch, the sights, the taste of ecstasy as they strove to please and be pleased.

Nathan gripped her hips, and Brenna, eyes closed and back arched, rode him toward the sky. The tempo increased with their breathing. Propping her hands on his chest, Brenna curled her nails into his shoulders, and it was the rapt intensity of her expression as much as anything that drove Nathan on until, with a small shriek, she stiffened above him. Her muscles spasmed around him. Her gripping urgency spilled him over the edge of need and into the kind folds of utopia. She collapsed onto his chest, panting softly against his shoulder. Their hearts thrummed against each other like ancient war drums, and in the background, a snowy owl called again, like the lullaby of a simpler time.

Eventually, able to breathe, to move, even to think a few rudimentary thoughts, Nathan kissed Brenna's shoulder. "So, did it work?"

"Huh?" she said, her tone groggy.

"Did it work? Are you cured? No more of that…you know…" He exhaled, still trying to catch his breath. "That nasty attraction stuff."

"Oh." She was still panting slightly, but managed to ease off him enough to glance shyly into his face. "Yeah. I'm sure it did. I'm…" She cleared her throat. "I'm fine now."

"Good." He ran his hand down the steep slope of her waist, felt her shiver violently against him and almost, *almost* grinned.

"Well…" She sat up, sounding businesslike but slightly breathless. "I suppose we should get dressed."

"After a swim."

"What?" she asked, but he was already on his feet and tugging her up after him.

"We're all cured now, so we might as well enjoy a swim."

"But—" She sounded slightly panicked, so he bent and lifted her into his arms. Her skin felt like warm satin against his naked body.

"Just to wash off," he said and carried her into the water.

The waves lapped up to his thighs and higher, over his buttocks and onto hers. He waded deeper and finally let her legs slip into the water. She tried to step away, and he intended to let her do it. But damn…the moon was still out and he had to kiss her. She resisted for a moment, but just when she was starting to soften, he let her go.

"Come on," he said. "There's something I want you to see."

He swam downstream a ways, and she followed until finally he saw what he was looking for. Swimming over to the huge boulder, he climbed up its smooth face to perch on the edge and urge her up beside him.

She came finally and they stood up together, gazing downstream where the moon glistened off the water like a thousand diamonds and the land seemed to roll away forever. A magical night in a magical place.

Finally, they made their way back to shore. Their clothes were much more reluctant to get on than to get off. But they managed it with some effort. The ride home was quiet. They turned their horses out to pasture and headed for the house. Brenna turned off the alarm system and let them in, but when she reached up to flip on the light, Nathan stopped her.

"I like the dark," he said softly and kissed her.

"Nathan..." She breathed his name against his lips. "I thought—"

"Right. I know. It's out of our systems." He pushed back her hair, heavy and damp. "We're just buddies now." Looping an arm around her back, he pulled her an inch closer. "So surely I can give you a friendly kiss." He kissed her again, slowly this time, lingeringly, letting his tongue sweep the swell of her bottom lip. "Can't I?"

"Umm..." She felt limp in his arms. "Sure."

He smiled and, reaching out, took her hand. "Come on. I'll escort you to your room."

Moonlight streamed onto her bed, picking out a few colors of the patchwork counterpane and casting the rest in moonbeam shadows.

"Better get out of those damp clothes," he said.

"I—"

"Here," he said. "I'll help you."

"Nathan, I think—"

"Just buddies," he said and reaching for her buttons, peeled her shirt away. The sight of her breasts in the moon-

light was almost his undoing, but he kept his tone brusque.
"Lie down."

"What?"

He tossed back the blankets on her bed. "Lie down. I'll
help with your pants."

To his everlasting gratitude, she did so, lying back on the
bed, with the moonlight soft and silver upon her. He untied
her shoes and pulled them off. Then he unsnapped her jeans
and finally tossed them on the floor.

"There. Slide in."

She did so and he swept the covers over her. He meant to
leave then, to give her a chance to dream about the hours
just past, to remember the beauty of their time together. To
realize how right they were together. He'd just kiss her good-
night and then go. Bending sideways, he brushed his lips
against hers. But drawing away was more difficult than an-
ticipated. He did so with great effort.

"Good night," he breathed, determined to make her realize her mistake by his absence.

"Good night." Her voice was whisper soft. So soft that
he *had* to lean closer to hear. And once he was closer, it
seemed so right to brush his lips across hers just once more.
When he drew away this time he was breathing hard and
starting to sweat. The upside was that her small fists were
curled into his shirt with darling ferocity.

He smiled inside. That was just where he wanted her—
needy, achy, lonely. He'd leave now, give her time.

"I've got to go," he said, but his tone didn't sound good.
Rather like a parched man left too long in the sun.

"Nathan." She breathed his name.

"What?"

She paused, seeming to fight a battle with herself.
"Maybe...maybe twice would be okay."

Oh God, yes. Yes, yes, yes, yes, yes, his body screamed.
But his head reprimanded him. "I'd like to..." More than
anything on earth! "But I think you're right. We have to set
boundaries. It's out of our systems now. I don't want to be
the death of your dream. You've worked so hard."

"Hard..." She pulled him closer, her fists still clenched in his shirt. He tried to resist, but she was really strong, he told himself. Her lips touched his. "Hard's good."

He allowed one brief kiss—one brief, drawn out, hotter-than-hell, curl your toes kiss.

"No. O'Shay...really." He made a feeble attempt to pull away, but just at that second, her hand slipped beneath his shirt. Her fingers felt like heaven against his taut muscles, and dammit, even the moonlight was against him.

With a martyred sigh, he lowered his body to hers and kissed her.

THE DAYS HURRIED BY in a wild rush of teasing and laughter, of long midnight talks and late-morning breakfasts.

Brenna tried to feel guilty, to remember her duties, her profession. But each time a smidgen of guilt crept in, Nathan would kiss her, or touch her hand, or look at her with his maple syrup eyes, and all would be forgotten.

They made love on the butcher block kitchen counter, in the oversized bathtub, and once in the attic, while supposedly searching for misplaced cowboy boots.

Brenna told herself she should be ashamed, but try as she might, she couldn't conjure up even a modicum of worthy guilt. So she told herself she was doing the right thing— getting him out of her system. But with each day that passed, he seemed more and more a part of her life, a part of her well-being, a part of *her*.

Weeks flew by, although Brenna couldn't say how many.

It was on a lazy Wednesday afternoon that Nathan decided Nuf needed a bath. Certain she didn't want to get involved in the argument between the two of them, Brenna declined the offer to assist him. But being near Nathan under any circumstances was preferable to being apart from him, and finally she was drawn into the melee. They emerged from the bathroom only slightly wetter than the cat, spattered with soapsuds and laughing too hard to actually find the tom who had darted, soaking and furious, toward the kitchen.

Nathan finally trailed him by his slippery path of water

and Brenna followed. The kitchen, she noticed, looked much as they had left it the night before when they'd been too distracted by miscellaneous body parts to tidy up. The truth was, neither of them were great housekeepers, and were it not for Tyrel's ancient housekeeper, Pansy, who came once a week to do a mercy cleaning, the place would probably have been condemned long ago.

"There he is," Brenna said, spying the tawny cat couched behind a spattered mixing bowl. She noticed his flattened ears and less-than-ecstatic expression. "I think Nuf has had enough."

Nathan laughed. "Geez, you're clever, O'Shay," he said, watching the cat. "Catch him and I'll do something special for you."

His hand touched the small of her back, and like Pavlov's dog, every nerve ending in her immediately started to hum.

"Something special," she said, turning toward him.

"Yeah." He raised his brows, then let his gaze skim the cluttered counter. "With the cooking oil." His fingers snuck beneath her blouse and made an intriguing little circle on her back.

She locked her knees and guessed, "You'll make fried chicken?"

"Not exactly," he said, and leaning closer, whispered in her ear. Her face felt warm and her hormones dizzying.

"Think you can catch him?" Nathan murmured, kissing her ear.

"Olive oil or corn?" she asked, sighing as she closed her eyes to the luscious feelings.

"Olive," he whispered.

She moaned slightly as his kisses trailed lower, then with a brave effort, turned away. "Well, for *olive oil*," she murmured. "Come here, cat. You're about to be sacrificed for the good of—"

But her words stopped dead. "Nathan," she whispered, barely able to breathe. "Where did that paper come from?"

He moved closer again, his fingers light against her skin. But her flesh had turned cold.

"Nathan! It's a letter!"

He straightened, his hands going still and his body tense. "Where?"

"By the flour bin."

They moved toward the counter together, their fingers somehow clasped between their tense bodies.

It was written on a plain sheet of narrow ruled paper ripped from a spiral notebook and said simply, "You're too damned lucky."

THE POLICE CAME, ASKED QUESTIONS, took the letter, searched the house for any clues, came up with nothing, and left.

Night settled in.

"I think you should hire someone else," Brenna said. The living room, which usually seemed so warm and friendly, suddenly felt chill and empty. "Another bodyguard." She rose to her feet and paced the length of the room, crossing the Navaho rug where they'd made love only two days before. The memory haunted her now. Had someone watched them? Had someone been standing in the shadows, planning evil? "Several bodyguards."

Nathan followed her with his gaze from the settle upholstered in hunter green. "Wouldn't they kind of cramp our style?"

She turned on him in wild frustration and biting fear. "What the hell's wrong with you, Fox?"

He shrugged and grinned a little, though his posture seemed stiff. "I'm horny?" Her jaw dropped and he laughed as he rose to his feet. "Listen—"

"No!" She snapped the word at him. "You listen. Someone's threatening your life. Someone was here. In this house. Someone—"

"They didn't threaten my life. They just—" he shrugged again, but his brow furrowed "—left a note."

"In your house! In your kitchen! They snuck past the security system. That means they know all about you. They've been watching your every move."

Nathan shook his head. "Maybe I forgot to turn it on." He smiled. "I've been a little distracted, you know," he said and leaned closer to kiss her.

She jerked away, terror and guilt spurring through her. "No more."

"What?"

"We won't be distracted anymore," she said. "You'll stay inside and wear a safety vest. I'll hire extra guards and a private detective. We'll find out—"

"No."

"Nathan—"

"No," he repeated softly. "This is me." He motioned toward the things around him. "This is what I am. I've given up enough for my career. I'm not going to give this up, too."

She ground her teeth. "So you'll give up your life!"

"My life!" He yelled the words, then pivoted away to yank his fingers through his hair. "No one has actually threatened me, O'Shay. There've just been a few letters. That's all."

"Threatening letters!"

"Threatening!" he scoffed. "We don't know they're threatening. Maybe they're just pranks."

"Pranks. Who—"

"I don't know who. I've met a million people in the past ten years. It could be any one of them. Someone I've played a trick on. Someone I went to school with. Someone who's seen me on the news, read about me in the paper, met me backstage."

"You're right," she said, managing to calm her voice. "It could be anyone, and that's why you've got to be more careful. Cancel any public appearances. Cut down on your—"

"No." His voice was calm now too. "I won't do it."

"Please." It seemed she wasn't above pleading. She bit her lip, trying to retain some pride, to remember why she had first met him. But it was no use. Their relationship was no longer even recognizable as that of an employer and employee. "Please. If you won't do it for yourself, will you do

it for me?'' she asked shamelessly. ''Because I...'' She
stopped, breathless, hopeless, terrified.

''Because what?'' he asked.

''Please,'' she whispered.

He stared at her, his eyes hard, and then, silent and angry,
he turned away and left the house.

15

"SEVEN POINT TWO SECONDS." The announcer's voice boomed over the loudspeaker. "Let's hear it for North Dakota's own Fox brothers. Nathan and Tyrel."

Several thousand fans screamed.

Brenna plugged one ear and spoke into her headset, her gaze never leaving Nathan as he waved to his fans.

"They'll be leaving the arena in just a few seconds. Make sure the exit is clear. I want two men at the gate and five lining each side of the barrier between Nathan and the crowd at all times."

Nathan kneed Lula forward and loosened his lariat enough to flip it off the steer's horns. Tyrel did the same, freeing the steer's hind legs. The animal shook his head and trotted irritably toward the exit.

With an additional wave, the Fox brothers left the arena.

Brenna followed along the steel railing, trotting to keep up and giving orders into her headset all the while. Near the corral where the bulls milled, she saw Shauna and Sarge and a few boys from the band, but she ignored them and managed to reach the exit just as Nathan did. Pushing through the crowd with some effort, she nodded to a beefy security man who held the mob at bay and hurried along beside the brothers' horses.

In less than sixty seconds they had reached their stalls. Nathan stepped smoothly out of the saddle. "Think you got enough security, O'Shay?"

She ignored him and spoke into her headset again to one of the men she'd hired against Nathan's will. "Well, tell them to *figure out* when he rides next. I want to know what bull, what chute, what time. Got it?''

"Maybe you better find out what color bull I drew," Nathan said.

She turned toward him, anger shot through her. "If you don't want security, Fox, don't take risks."

"Risks!" He snorted. "You think putting syrup on my pancakes is too risky."

They stood faced off, surrounded by a half dozen guards. In the past week, they'd barely spoken ten words to each other. But now, standing so close to him, Brenna felt all those hot, distracting emotions rush back in like a curling tide. She held them at bay with a tight rein.

"You've done the team roping, Fox," she said, careful to keep her tone level. "Go home now."

He stared at her, and for one wildly hopeful moment, she thought he might agree. But finally he shook his head. "I've got a bull to ride, O'Shay."

She tried to remain strong, but despite her best efforts, she could not. "Please," she said softly.

"I gotta do this. You, of all people, should understand that." He took a step toward her, but she regained her composure before he could touch her.

"Fine," she said, and turning away, snapped a half-dozen orders into her headset.

The time passed like a speedy dirge, with Brenna tailing Nathan every moment. Each time he turned around she was staring him in the face, but his glare did nothing to make her back off.

The afternoon wound down.

"Bull riding!" the announcer boomed, his voice dramatic. "The most dangerous sport in America today."

Brenna ignored the knot in her stomach and ran her hands down Nathan's rigging one more time. Made of thick cowhide, it felt solid and whole.

"Want to check it after we cinch it on him?" a cowboy asked, nodding to a red bull confined to a narrow, high-walled chute.

Brenna couldn't tell if the cowboy was being facetious or honest. But it didn't matter, for she was far past being either intimidated or embarrassed. "Yes," she said, and handed him the rigging. Walking over to the chute, she looked through the bars. The animal was as big as a bus with twelve-inch horns and a nose that bowed out like a wildebeest's. He turned toward her and glared through red-rimmed eyes. He was sweating, and there was a tiny smudge of blood on his shoulder where one of the other bulls must have scraped him with a horn, but despite all that, he seemed quiet enough.

Brenna prayed that looks weren't deceiving.

The first two cowboys mounted their bulls and completed their rides unscathed. Brenna refused to look. A thousand carefully chosen words ran through her mind as she watched Nathan step over the top of the chute to straddle the bull's back. But in the end she could think of only one thing to say.

"Please be careful." The words were whispered, but he turned to her nevertheless, his lips canted into that heart-stopping half smile that was so uniquely his.

"I love you," he said softly and settled onto the bull's corded back.

Brenna's mouth fell open, her heart raced like a runaway horse, but she was given no time to respond.

The chute gate swung wide. The bull turned his head toward the opening and stared. The crowd was expectantly silent. But suddenly a cowboy leaned over the chute, flapping a hat.

The bull started, and suddenly, like a mad spring hare, he launched from confinement. Bucking erratically, he thundered toward the side rail and crashed into the fence. Nathan was tossed sideways like a tortured rag doll, but he managed to hang on.

The crowd gasped. The bull was already turning. Staggering away, he began to spin madly, throwing his body in every direction like a crazed dervish. But suddenly, without a moment's warning, he collapsed on his side, pinning his rider's leg beneath him.

"Nathan!" Brenna screamed his name. Sarge reached for her, but she yanked out of his grip. She was over the fence in an instant, but the bull was up just as quickly, leaving his rider behind.

Foam dribbled from the animal's gaping mouth as he turned his wild eyes to Nathan.

"No!" she screamed again, racing across the arena, oblivious to everything but Nathan's final words. He loved her. He loved her.

From her right, a clown tried to snare her, but she dodged past him.

Nathan had gained his feet. The bull lowered his head.

"Here! Here!" Brenna screamed and waved her arms, drawing the bull's attention.

He turned his eyes to her, tossed his head once, and charged.

Brenna pivoted away, heart pounding. Hoofbeats thundered behind her. Terror rode her. The rest was a blur of colors and pain. She felt her ribs creak, saw the world fly by below her. And there, seeming a universe away, was Nathan hanging onto the bull's tail.

Damn him. She was supposed to be protecting *him*, Brenna thought, and fell headfirst into oblivion.

"YOU'RE AWAKE," NATHAN SAID, barely able to breathe for the hot tide of relief that rushed through him. The bull had only hit her once, then had turned in an attempt to remove Nathan from his tail. In moments, the animal had been shagged from the arena and the ambulance had arrived almost immediately. Still, it seemed that a lifetime had passed since he'd watched her fall.

"Nathan." She breathed his name. "You're all right?"

"Sure." He squeezed her hand and longed to pull her into his arms. But bull riding had taught him too much about internal injuries to risk it. "I got you as a bodyguard, don't I?"

"You were supposed to run."

"What?" His eyes stung, but crying seemed kind of sissy, so he decided not to.

"When I diverted the bull, you were supposed to run."

"Oh. Sorry." He tried for a self-effacing grin. It didn't come off so good. "You should have said so."

"Thought you'd know."

"You'll have to move back," said a paramedic. "We're going to take her to the hospital."

"I'm going with her."

"But your leg—"

"I'm going with her," Nathan repeated.

Her gurney was lifted from the ground and slid into the ambulance. Nathan's leg hurt like hell as he climbed in beside her, but he ignored the pain. Swooning was cute when *she* did it, but didn't seem right for his macho character.

The doors closed behind them.

"You hurt your leg," she said.

"It's been busted before."

"You broke it?"

She grimaced as she tried to sit up. He pushed her back down.

"Can't you give her something for the pain?" Nathan asked, worry sluicing through him.

"I was just going to do that," said the paramedic.

"No!" Brenna objected, but the syringe had already been emptied into her IV. "I've got to guard you." Her eyes looked desperate.

"Relax," Nathan pleaded. "Let me take care of you this once."

"Your leg…" She looked like she was going to cry.

He tightened his grip on her hand. "They'll take care of it at the hospital. I'll be close. Please, don't worry."

But he could tell she did, for she was fighting to stay alert.

They turned a corner. The ambulance came to a halt and the doors swung open. She was lifted out and rolled away.

Nathan hurried to keep up.

"What the hell are you doing, Fox? Get your butt in a

wheelchair.'' Sarge's voice was gruff as he hustled over from his car with Shauna right behind him.

Brenna lifted her lids with a stubborn effort. ''Watch Nathan,'' she rasped.

''Everything'll be all right. Nate's tough,'' Shauna said.

Brenna turned her gaze messily to Sarge, and he nodded. ''Don't worry,'' he said, his expression hard. ''I won't mess up this time.''

STRANGE IMAGES BUZZED through Brenna's mind like disembodied butterflies. Flashes of reality mixed in a world of make-believe—bulls in clown pants, a rodeo in the bathroom, Nathan riding a platinum record down a twisted trail. The world leveled off, leaving her with a few bright images, Nathan's smile, the sound of his voice, the touch of his hand. Laughter and sunlight and silly lyrics to beautiful songs.

Brenna smiled and opened her eyes. The room was dark, but even without her glasses she could tell she was in a hospital. Memories rushed back in a painful wave.

Nathan! She sat up. A hundred myriad pains sparked through her. She gasped for breath and remembered more.

Nathan was safe. Sarge and Shauna had promised to protect him. She carefully lay back down. They were two of his oldest friends and would take care of things until she could. What she must do now was think. Figure things out. Someone had left a letter in Nathan's kitchen. Who? And if he planned Nathan any harm, why hadn't he done something at the rodeo? It seemed the obvious place, what with the bulls—

Brenna's mind stumbled to a halt. The bulls! Her brain spun into action. The bull, sweaty, absolutely still in his chute. Why would he run into the rail, unless... The smear of blood on his shoulder! Could he have been given an injection? Drugged? By whom? How?

Answers jumbled in her head.

''Nathan!'' she gasped. The world spun momentarily as she swung her feet to the floor. But she focused on the door. There was no time to lose! Not an instant! She hustled, chilled and panicked, into the hall. The light struck her eyes. Where was he? Which room?

"Nathan!" She pushed a door open and switched on a light. The bed was empty. She hurried to the next room. A blond woman sat up groggily when she opened the door.

Brenna turned away. Where? Her gaze fell on a chair next to a room door. She spun toward it. The floor wavered as she rushed across it. The door swung open beneath her hand. She lurched inside.

"Shauna!" Brenna tried to scream. It came out as a squeak and stopped in the middle.

From beside Nathan's bed, a bulldog face turned toward her. A syringe was held in rubber-gloved hands.

"Sarge," she whispered.

His expression of shock turned to anger. "What the hell are you doing here?"

"Sarge," she said again, stunned to immobility. "Why?"

"He's a user." His tone was flat.

"What?" She shook her head, trying to rid herself of this new nightmare. But she couldn't wake up.

"He was nothing. Just a hick farm kid with a grin and a guitar. Shauna and me, we were the show, but Fox...he knows how to use folks." He took a step toward her. "Don't he?"

She backed away, shaking her head.

"Don't believe me? You should. But women always fall for him. Shauna learned her lesson. The letters were her idea. But you figured that out, didn't you? She wrote them, then sent them off from different places. Except the last two. I slipped the one into his hotel room just to see the look on her face. Tipped it right out of my hat." He grinned.

"Then the accidents—"

Sarge laughed. "The accidents were accidents. But, God, it was fun to watch him pretend he wasn't worried, and all the time he was sweating like a pig. I wasn't about to let him die before his time. I had it planned so perfect. I could see the headlines 'The Fox dies as public as he lives.' But..."

He shrugged, lifting the syringe. "I always have a backup plan."

"Why?" Brenna whispered.

"Any idea what it's like to have your dream pulled out from under you? But maybe you do, 'cause you're not really a bodyguard, are you, Brenna Theresa O'Shay?"

"You're the one who called Bartman about me."

He chuckled. "Jesus, how I laughed when he picked you. Was just like him to fall for a woman, and just like a woman to fall for him. Shauna was just as stupid, till she hooked a bigger fish. She's a user too. Never thought she'd have the guts to kill him, though. But I guess I was wrong, 'cause look." He held up the syringe and grinned. "Her fingerprints are all over this."

"You're framing her," Brenna said.

He chuckled. "You're smarter than I gave you credit for at first. But you don't have to go down with this, O'Shay. It'll be our secret. You can even be the one that busts Shauna. And I'll give you a first-rate recommendation."

"You're insane."

"I'm inspired," he contradicted. "There is a difference."

"They'll know Shauna wasn't here."

"She *was* here," he said. "Seconds ago. Same time the nurse saw me go into the john. Hospitals are terrible understaffed these days. Shauna bitches about it all the time. Nobody saw me come out of the john or come in here. They'll all think Shauna did it. Jilted lover and all that. Her syringe." He lifted it as evidence. "Epinephrine for the bull. Pentothal for Fox. All taken from Shauna's hospital. She'll deny it, of course. But it'll be obvious, specially when I tell them 'bout her letters. Fox'll be dead. I'll be grieving. I tried so hard to protect him. Everyone knows I did. Only wild card is you, O'Shay," he said and took a step toward her. "And he's used you just like he did the rest of us."

"This'll never work," she said, backing away.

"Why? Because of Fox?" He nodded toward the bed. "He's a lucky bastard, but he's pumped to the gills with painkillers. He won't wake up. All I got to worry about is you," he said, and lunged.

Brenna tried to dodge, to strike, to do something, but her mind was numb and her muscles frozen. Sarge's hand closed over her throat. The syringe darted nearer.

But suddenly there was a crash behind him.

Sarge pivoted about, but Nathan was already swinging. The telephone crashed against Sarge's skull. He flopped sideways, but came up with a roar, syringe held like a knife as he lunged forward. Nathan jumped back, but his splint crashed into the leg of the bed and he fell.

"No!" Brenna yelled and spinning round, slammed her bare heel into Sarge's cranium. He reeled sideways. She gave him no time to recover. Gripping both hands together, she swung her fists. They caught him in the left ear. He went down in a clatter of bottles and bedpans.

Gasping in pain, Brenna sprang at him from all fours and hit him square on the back. He crumbled like a house of cards and lay still.

The door sprang open. Brenna spared one quick glance over her shoulder, but remained just as she was, her knees on his back and her hands in his collar. Three people stood in the doorway, their mouths open, their eyes wide.

"Call the police!" she gasped.

The trio remained staring with open mouths.

Brenna scowled. Now that the excitement was over, pain was snapping through her ribcage like electricity through a wire. "Call the police," she snapped.

The only woman in the group spun into the hall in search of a telephone. The men continued to stare.

"What's the matter with you? Haven't you seen a bodyguard before?"

Nathan, still sprawled on his back at the foot of the bed, cleared his throat. "I think they maybe haven't seen that much of a bodyguard before," he said.

She tried to form a question, but he explained before she managed.

"These hospital gowns weren't made for your life-style, O'Shay."

She snatched the back of her gown closed and sputtered, "Sweet—"

"What's going on here?" A dark-haired man pushed his way into the room. Four others followed him.

"Shamus!" Brenna gasped, still crouched like a tree frog atop Sarge.

"Are you Fox?" the closest man asked.

Nathan scooted to his feet as answers to unasked questions tumbled into his head. The blond guy was the man who'd harassed O'Shay in Charlotte, and Nathan had seen the dark-haired fellow flat on his back in a coliseum in Omaha. They were her brothers. He was sure of it.

"I'm Fox," Nathan said, sizing up the nearest brother. He was built like an overzealous wrestler, and looked fit enough to wrangle the bull that had just tromped Nathan. "What do you want?"

"I want to know what kind of man hides behind a woman," Shamus said.

Nathan shrugged and tried a grin, but even that slight movement sent a spasm of pain through him. "I guess that'd be me."

Shamus snorted. "Guess so. Come on, Brenna. We're going home."

"Brenna!" Nathan said, delighted to finally hear her name. "That's even better than Bambi."

Brenna sent him an exasperated look before turning to her brothers. "Give it up, Shamus," she said. "I'm not going home."

"The hell you're not. Daddy told me before he died to take care of you and that's what I'm going to do," he said and moved closer.

But Nathan stepped in between them, his hands raised in a symbol of peace. "She said she's not going," he said.

"Get out of my way."

"You're going to have to make me," Nathan said, barely able to balance on his splint. "But I gotta tell you something first. Your sister's a damn good bodyguard. And if that's what she wants to do that's what she's going to do."

"Get out of the way."

"Well, I would," Nathan said. "But if I do she's going to kick your sorry behind, and I don't want to see you hurt…'cause I'm hoping to make you my brother-in-law."

"What?" Shamus snarled.

"What?" Brenna gasped.

Nathan turned toward her. "Marry me, O'Shay," he said.

"But what about…" She shook her head, looking shocked.

"You want to guard bodies, go ahead," Nathan said. "Mine or someone else's. I understand dreams. I won't stand in your way. Just…" For a moment, he forgot how to form words. "Will you…marry me?"

"Yes!" she croaked and, stumbling over Sarge's flaccid legs, swooned prettily in Nathan's arms.

"O'SHAY."

Brenna sat up with a start. "What—"

"Shh," Nathan whispered. The hospital room was dark again. A full day had passed since Sarge had been incarcerated and her brothers had left for Mississippi.

"What are you doing here?" she whispered.

"Wanted to talk to you."

"You're supposed to be in bed."

"'Bout time you asked," he said, and half dragging his new cast across the floor, crawled in beside her.

"You can't—"

"Shh," he said. "I couldn't sleep. Questions keep chasing each other through my head."

In the dim light, his expression looked vulnerable and wounded. She reached for him, drawing him close. "I wish I had the answers. Your oldest friend. How could he do it?" She touched Nathan's face. It felt warm and sandpaper-rough beneath her fingertips.

He exhaled softly. "Jealousy, I guess. We were a team a couple of lifetimes ago. Sarge and Shauna and me. I can't believe…'' He squeezed his eyes closed, but opened them in a moment. ''Shauna confessed her part about the letters. Sent them just to spook me. Didn't expect Sarge to leave them in my hotel. In my kitchen. Never meant any real harm. Didn't know what Sarge was planning.''

Silence filled the room.

''Guess it's the truth. 'Cause it looks like he was trying to frame her. The police found a syringe in her glove compartment. It had a drop of the same stuff he tried to kill me with.'' He cleared his throat. ''It had her fingerprints all over it.''

''I'm sorry,'' Brenna whispered.

''Yeah, well, at least he hates her just as much as he does me.''

''How could he hate you? How could they—''

''Shh.'' Nathan gently touched a finger to her lips. ''Maybe I'm a cold-hearted son of a bitch, 'cause it wasn't *those* questions that were hounding me. I was wondering…are you sure?''

''Sure?''

''That you want to marry me. I know it wasn't fair to ask you when you were all doped up, half-naked in front of your brothers and God and everyone. But I didn't think…''

''I wasn't half-naked.''

''Well…'' He smoothed his fingers down her throat to her collarbone. ''Not your best half anyway. Still, it was pretty intriguing. I thought I was going to have to chase the male nurses away with my crutches.''

She cleared her throat and tried to crush her embarrassment. ''Would you have?''

Leaning forward ever so slightly, he pressed a gentle kiss to the corner of her mouth. Tingling feelings of utopia floated through her.

''Would I have what?'' he murmured, his lips only a breath away from her ear, his touch feather soft against her neck as he brushed her hair back.

She closed her eyes at the glorious sensations. ''Would you have chased them off for me?''

"Well, I don't know." His hand traveled past her shoulder, found the bare strip of skin down the middle of her back and followed it leisurely. "My south side doesn't look as good in a hospital gown as yours does."

He gently stroked the curve of her buttocks. Feelings distracted her, but uncertainty niggled at her mind, so she tried to keep focused.

"Are *you* sure, Fox?" she asked breathlessly.

He was silent for a moment. She could feel his gaze, warm as a spring breeze on her face, but she refused to open her eyes, lest she see uncertainty in his expression.

"Am I sure I want to marry you?" he asked.

She nodded, because her throat was suddenly and foolishly all clogged up, and she doubted her ability to speak.

"I've been sure for a long time, O'Shay."

Joy snapped through her, but she carefully contained it, wanting, *needing* to know the truth. She forced her eyes open, meeting his.

"Really? Since when?"

"Do you remember when you said—" he paused as if recalling the exact words "—my name is B. T. O'Shay?"

She exhaled with a small huff, exasperated both by his poor attempt at her accent and his words. "That was the first time we met."

"Yeah," he said and kissed her throat.

"You're kidding me," she decided, but the words were only a murmur, lost in a rush of hot feelings that made her want to arch into him, to kiss him, to forget all about talking.

But nevertheless, he spoke. "Yeah, I'm kidding," he admitted. "I didn't know for sure until a couple days later—when you jumped Ian in the hall."

"You knew you wanted to marry me when I made a fool of myself?"

"Exactly."

She gave him a little punch to the ribs. He grunted, rubbed the spot, and grinned. "You should have seen yourself, O'Shay," he said. "Beautiful and sassy and..." He paused, his expression going sober. "And worried about me. Really caring about *me*. In this business that's not so easy to find."

She loved him. So much. "That's when you knew? Really?"

"Yeah," he said and sighed. "I tried to be patient. Tried to give you space. But I'm damned tired of being your buddy, O'Shay. I don't know if I can go back to that. But if you need more time—"

"Yes," she whispered.

"Yes what?"

"I'm sure I want to marry you. But only if you call me Brenna."

"Brenna," he whispered and loosened the tie at the back of her neck. The gown slipped languidly sideways. His lips touched her bare shoulder, igniting a thousand wild feelings. "Are you ready to shock the hospital staff?"

"More than ready," she said and kissed him.

Look for a new and exciting series from Harlequin!

HARLEQUIN
Duets™

Two __new__ full-length novels in one book, from some of your favorite authors!

Starting in May, each month we'll be bringing you two new books, each book containing two brand-new stories about the lighter side of love! Double the pleasure, double the romance, for less than the cost of two regular romance titles!

Look for these two new Harlequin Duets™ titles in May 1999:

Book 1:
WITH A STETSON AND A SMILE
by Vicki Lewis Thompson
THE BRIDESMAID'S BET
by Christie Ridgway

Book 2:
KIDNAPPED? by Jacqueline Diamond
I GOT YOU, BABE by Bonnie Tucker

2 GREAT STORIES BY 2 GREAT AUTHORS FOR 1 LOW PRICE!

Don't miss it! Available May 1999 at your favorite retail outlet.

HARLEQUIN®
Makes any time special.™

LOVE & LAUGHTER™

Tell us a funny romantic story, we asked.

Jennifer McKinlay told a great one and won
$1,000 in the Love & Laughter contest.

Up, up and away!

"Honey, when are we going to get married?"

"I'm not ready," Bob answered. Bob, my beau, my
love, my commitment phobe.

After four years of dating and three years of
cohabiting, this chorus and refrain had become our
song. Feeling desperate, I consulted my backlog of
Cosmopolitans. Sure enough, they stated emphatically to
give him an ultimatum, but be ready to back it up. Oh,
dear! Being a generous soul, I gave him one year.

The year ticked by. We continued our song, but now I
had a new verse—"A ring or else." This did not have the
desired effect of changing his tune.

Halloween came. I got bupkiss. Thanksgiving came.
Nada. Hey, I'd have been happy to find a ring in my
stuffing. Christmas came. I got a watch. Great, now I
could really watch time pass me by. I gave up.

My beau is a quirky artist, and I knew I had to
forgive his commitment-phobic ways in order to remain
friends. And he is my best friend. So on New Year's Eve
when he asked me to help him with a photo shoot at
dawn, I agreed. Insane, I know.

Not being a morning person and suffering from
the flu, I felt too lousy to shower that day. I slapped
on a baseball cap and my best clothes-that-should-be-
rags outfit. When we arrived at our destination in the
middle of the desert, Bob went to chat with his client
while I sat in our truck with a tissue up my nose,
nursing my illness.

Upon introduction, I discovered that his client was a hot air balloonist. Ah! Now this made sense to me. Bob is petrified of heights, and I realized he was going to need me to take the pictures for him.

As the sun lightened the sky, Bob and I scrambled into the rising basket of our enormous red-and-black balloon. There were twenty balloons taking off around us, and I was snapping photos as if I was working for *Life* magazine.

Bob, poor thing, was too busy clutching the supports, his head tucked under the burner and a cap of ash covering his hair, to observe much of the view about us. Our pilot kept me busy with photos while he talked on his radio to our road crew below. (They follow you in case you crash. How thoughtful.)

We had floated for half an hour when Bob released his death grip on the supports to nudge me.

"Honey, what's that down there?" he asked, looking green.

I glanced down and darn near fell out of the basket. Our road crew had parked in the middle of nowhere and they were holding an enormous banner that read...

JENN, WILL YOU MARRY ME?

Being the rational woman I am, I yelled, "Oh, my God!" and snapped a photo of it.

"Well?" Bob asked.

"Yes!" I blubbered.

We kissed and hugged, and he pulled out the most beautiful ring I'd ever seen. It fit perfectly.

When I asked Bob later what had possessed him to propose in a hot air balloon, he said, "Because I wanted you to know that I meant it."

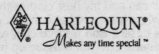

HARLEQUIN®
Makes any time special ™

LOVE & LAUGH

INTO APRIL!

#65 50 WAYS TO LURE YOUR LOVER
Julie Kistler

When reporter Mabel Ivey lands a job at *Real Men* magazine, she's thrilled. As part of her first assignment, she finds herself the subject of a glamorous makeover. Suddenly, she's discovering what it's like to be a sex object. She has to admit it's fun—until the man of her dreams begins pursuing her. Then Mabel has to discover whether he's in love with the *new* her...or the *real* her.

#66 SWEET REVENGE?
Kate Hoffmann

Tess Ryan has seen her sister Lucy through countless broken relationships. But even *she* can't believe Lucy's crazed obsession with getting even with her last boyfriend. Besides, it's hard for Tess to be sympathetic when she's just fallen head over heels for the first time in her life. Still, she has to save the poor guy from her sister's wrath. Especially when she discovers that Andrew Wyatt, the new love of Tess's life, is the poor guy in question...

Chuckles available now:

#63 FROM HERE TO MATERNITY
Cheryl Anne Porter
#64 HIS BODYGUARD
Lois Greiman

LOVE & LAUGHTER™